"I wasn't finished..."

"With what?" Catherine asked, all innocence, his hungry look and low raspy voice exciting her.

"Kissing you," Tony said, pulling her close. The way he took her mouth, possessive and demanding, accelerated more than her heartbeat.

It was thrilling. Her breasts brushed against his chest, her hardened nipples sensitive enough to make her breath catch. She squeezed her legs together as tightly as she could, needing the pressure, wanting so much more.

His hands tightened on her waist, and he lifted her up onto the center island. Their eyes were level now, and she could see the black of his widening pupils.

"Christ, you're beautiful," he whispered, then kissed her as he slid his hands underneath her dress, moving them up her thighs, which seemed to part of their own volition. "I've been thinking about this since the last time you were here," he said.

"Except this time, I intend to finish what I start."

Dear Reader,

I'm back writing about my favorite city in the world—New York! In this gently reimagined tale of Little Italy, five generations of the Paladino family have lived in their house on Mulberry Street since 1910. Now, they've got a thriving construction firm where three hot brothers, Tony, Luca and Dominic, work, live and love in the shrinking, old-fashioned world of close Italian families who seem to specialize in gossip.

In *Tempted in the City*, Tony Paladino meets a woman who is most definitely not one of their own. Catherine Fox works as a translator at the United Nations. After growing up in Europe, the daughter of diplomats, she's finally found the home she's always dreamed of in the heart of Little Italy.

Unfortunately, the Old Guard—a bunch of nosy neighbors who should know better—objects to this stranger remodeling one of the few single-family homes in the neighborhood.

Tony, on the other hand, loves everything about Cat. From the moment she hires his family to do the remodel, the two of them click in every way... especially in the bedroom.

It's supposed to be just a fling—until they finish the house. But life doesn't always follow a blueprint.

I hope you all fall in love with the Brothers Paladino in the hot NYC Bachelors series! I certainly have.

Ciao,

Jo Leigh

Jo Leigh

—

Tempted in the City

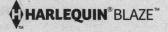

Recycling programs
for this product may
not exist in your area.

ISBN-13: 978-0-373-79912-1

Tempted in the City

Printed in U.S.A.

Jo Leigh is from Los Angeles and always thought she'd end up living in Manhattan. So how did she end up in Utah in a tiny town with a terrible internet connection, being bossed around by a houseful of rescued cats and dogs? What the heck, she says, predictability is boring. Jo has written more than forty-five novels for Harlequin. Visit her website at joleigh.com or contact her at joleigh@joleigh.com.

Books by Jo Leigh

Harlequin Blaze

Three Wicked Nights

One Breathless Night
One Sizzling Night
One Blazing Night

It's Trading Men

Choose Me
Have Me
Want Me
Seduce Me
Dare Me
Intrigue Me

To get the inside scoop on Harlequin Blaze and its talented writers, be sure to check out blazeauthors.com.

All backlist available in ebook format.

Visit the Author Profile page at Harlequin.com for more titles.

1

"WHERE THE HELL have you been?"

Tony Paladino stopped in his tracks as Gina, his cousin and the office manager at Paladino & Sons, came at him waving a wad of pink message slips. He held his hand up to stop her as he checked the text on his cell phone.

Sure enough, Rita wanted to meet later, after work. She was in town only for tonight, and he wasn't going to let anything get in the way of seeing her. He hadn't had sex in too damn long, and Rita was just the ticket. Uncomplicated, didn't even live in New York, and she wanted nothing from him but some hot action with a wave goodbye after. Perfect.

He answered her text in very few words, and the moment he hit Send, Gina pounced.

"You were supposed to be here two hours ago. Alex, the plumber on the Ortega job, says the whole system needs replacing from the ground up, and that was not in his budget, so he wants his money up front.

"Also, Sal is going crazy at Catherine Fox's house. He says she's insane and if you don't call him back right away, he's going to pack it up and go home."

"Well, that's just great." Tony shook his head. The hits just kept on coming.

"I'm not finished," Gina said. "The mayor's assistant is trying to get hold of your father to ask him to dinner as thanks for the remodel of his offices. And Leo's truck broke down in Park Slope so he hasn't gotten to the Walkers' brownstone yet. There's a bunch more, but those are the calls you need to get to right away."

"Sounds about right after the morning I've had. Thanks, Gina."

She put a hand on her hip and gave him the stink eye.

"Hey, I told you I had to go to Aunt Miriam's house."

"You were there this whole time?"

"She made me physically verify every item on her final punch list while the project manager drank coffee and ate biscotti, because suddenly *I'm* the only one she trusts."

"Oh. Well, it wouldn't have killed you to text me back."

"I forgot to turn my cell phone back on. But you're right. I'll try not to do that again. I tell you, Miriam is—"

"A lunatic with too much time on her hands." Gina gave him one of her best "all is forgiven" smiles when she handed him the messages. "I thought maybe you weren't so anxious to get here. This being the first day and all."

"Nah, why delay the inevitable?" he said, shrugging, though anxiety had tightened his chest a few times.

"Congratulations, Tony. You're going to do your father proud taking over the company. I left some files on his desk but that's it. I didn't touch anything. I figured you'd want to fix things up yourself."

"I don't think that office will ever feel like anything but Dad's. I'll do my best and we'll take it one day at a time. And by the way, let's stop with the pink slips, huh? We can do all of this on our tablets."

"Thank God," she said. "Chasing down you and your brothers is like herding cats. This way, I won't get blamed when the three of you screw up."

"Gee thanks," Tony said, slowly making his way past the reception area. "But I'm pretty sure we'll find a way to blame you, anyway."

Gina laughed. It made her look younger, prettier, although that might have been the result of her new hairstyle. It used to be dark and big, and now it was lighter and smaller. He liked it.

"Do me a favor? Call Leo. Make sure he's got his truck taken care of and see if Dom can get over to the Walker's place?"

She nodded, already dialing her cell phone.

Once in his office, Tony sat down in his father's black leather chair behind the massive oak desk and looked around the room. Everything about it reminded him that he had large shoes to fill. Joe had run Paladino & Sons Construction and Renovation for so many years the office still held a hint of the Aqua Net hair spray he swore he didn't use.

As the eldest son, Tony had been with the company since he'd graduated from NYU back in 2004. Unofficially, he'd been with the company since the minute he could walk. It wasn't the work that felt daunting. What scared him was being in charge of the Paladino legacy. Their name meant something. You wanted a job done right, on time and on budget, you called the Paladinos. They kept their word. They also kept the heart of New York's Little Italy intact in more ways than anyone who wasn't immediate family knew.

They'd looked out for the people in the nine blocks on the Lower East Side. Had done so since 1912, when the first Paladino had come over from Sicily.

At least—thank God—his father was still with them after last week's scare. Joe's second heart attack had been a near miss. But even with strict orders from his doctor to retire, Joe would probably sneak into the office from time to time. Not that Tony would blame him. Construction ran in the Paladinos' blood.

He called Sal, an old friend and one of their best project managers. He'd handled a lot of difficult clients in the past, so what was making him nuts about the Fox project?

"About time you called," Sal said after one ring. "Your client is insane."

"Why?"

"Okay, so she says we're supposed to avoid damaging anything that might be original to the house. Art deco, she says, that was the agreement. She wants it all restored, from tile work to crown moldings. First of all, there's nothing like that in the contract. Second, how are we supposed to know what the hell is original in this place? It was built in 1902. Look, Tony, I'm sorry to put this on you on your first day as boss, man, but you know the schedule we're running here, and there's a list of jobs a mile long waiting for me. So what do you want me to do?"

Tony opened his eyes. He hadn't even realized he'd been cringing. The Fox contract had been one of the last his father had done. He'd started making mistakes a couple months before that, and while Tony had caught most of them, he hadn't paid much attention to the Fox job because he trusted Sal. But this was a big project, a complete remodel from foundation to roof, and not something he could fix over the phone.

"Look, just keep working in the areas that aren't in question. I'll contact Catherine Fox and find out what she's talking about and get back to you, okay?"

"Okay. But, Tony, this needs to be settled by tomorrow. I have another job right in back of this one, and we're supposed to be taking down walls as soon as we get the nod from the inspectors."

"I know. I'll handle it."

"Yeah. And, Tony. I'm sorry about your dad."

"Thanks, Sal. He'll be okay." When Tony hung up, Gina stood at the edge of his door. "What about the whiteboard?"

The huge board was in the main office. It listed every job, its current stage and who was in charge of the operation. Joe hadn't been big on tech. He'd done things the way his father and grandfather had. Those methods had taken them through a lot of rocky financial years, kept them, their relatives, employees and all the regular subcontractors working when a lot of other companies had gone belly-up. Tony wasn't going to make too many changes at once.

"Why don't we leave it for now."

"So your dad will feel better when he sneaks back to visit?" Gina said, her fondness not hidden by the teasing words.

"Actually, yeah."

"Good thinking," she said.

"Hey, were my brothers here?"

Gina nodded.

"See if you can reschedule our meeting for tomorrow."

"Already done. Luca will be here for sure. Dom hasn't texted me back, but he'll make time. They were disappointed you weren't here, so they couldn't make a fuss out of you moving over to your dad's office. Dom brought doughnuts."

"Don't tell me he actually paid for them."

Gina laughed. "He got them from that silly Carveccio girl."

"Of course he did," Tony said, more to himself than Gina. He looked down at the other pink slips on the desk. The top message was from Angie, his ex-wife. He could put that off, but not for long. Better to get the last of the financial settlement over with, even if things would be tight until they got more caught up with their receivables. The Paladinos had always adjusted the family salaries to make their payments, and never thought of touching the money in the trust. Tony wasn't going to change that now.

The remaining five messages, everything from job snafus to a request for a radio interview, didn't need his attention today. He still had to call Alex, but first he had to get in touch with Catherine Fox and make sure they met ASAP. He had one chance to see Rita tonight, and he wasn't going to miss it.

"Little Italy, please, Grand and Lafayette." Catherine settled in the backseat of the yellow cab, reminding herself she had no control over the heavy New York traffic. To go from the United Nations building to her new home was exactly 5.3 miles, but it took at least twenty-five minutes to get there. If she was lucky.

She wasn't lucky today.

The whole construction debacle had come as a shock. Not just that the project manager had acted as if he knew nothing about her revised restoration plans, but that she'd accepted a verbal agreement in the first place.

It had been completely out of character, but there'd been something about Joseph Paladino that she'd trusted immediately. At the same time, she wasn't naive enough to think she didn't need the amendment in writing. This home meant everything to her. What had she been thinking?

God, she could just scream.

Now, instead of hashing things out with Joseph, she had to deal with his son. Everything about it smelled rotten. This major snafu had caused her to be late returning from lunch, which meant she'd need to go back to work later. Worse than that, it felt like a bait and switch, which she was going to nip right in the bud. Despite all the recommendations and exceptional reviews of Paladino & Sons, they were not going to play her for a fool.

There were other contractors, though she really hoped this was a mix-up and she hadn't been taken in by the very sincere-seeming Paladino, Sr. She of all people should be able to spot a con artist. Her job was dependent on her ability to read nuance and body language. But just in case, she'd already started to compile a list of alternatives.

They turned on Grand and she spotted Tony Paladino right away. Tall, dark haired and trim, he carried a black satchel and wore dark jeans and a white oxford shirt with no tie.

After paying the cabbie, she straightened her skirt as she approached where Tony stood facing her front door. The outside of the three-story town house was redbrick and beautiful, although there was definitely work to be done on her front stoop. Whether it would be done by this guy's company remained to be seen.

He turned upon hearing her heels on the uneven sidewalk. "Hello," he said, holding out his hand. "Tony Paladino."

She met his chestnut-brown eyes and her heart started beating harder. "Catherine Fox," she said, noting the strength of his handshake. "I must admit, I'm disappointed that your father couldn't be here."

"He would have been if he'd been able, I assure you."

She took out her key and slid it into the lock. It gave her the moment she needed to think about something other than the fact that Tony was an unexpectedly good-looking man. Catherine turned the key just as a distasteful thought occurred to her. This might be exactly what she'd feared. Was Mr. Charm here supposed to distract her long enough for them to renege and have her sign off?

The hell with that. They would finish the job, all right. Exactly to her specifications. Just as Joseph Paladino had promised.

A moment later they were inside. The ground floor was where most of the building supplies were spread out, so they had to make their way past scaffolds, tarps and exposed pipes. The focus so far had been on the foundation, electrical and plumbing, basic work about which she wasn't concerned. She led Tony up to the small suite she'd made her home base. It took up only a quarter of the second floor—which would eventually become her master suite and one guest room—but it was large enough for now.

Even though the work was loud and messy during the week, she hadn't been around for most of it, leaving her to get used to the old place on the nights and weekends. She had a makeshift bedroom, bathroom, kitchen and small sitting area where she could watch television.

She put her purse on the table by the entrance, reminding herself to keep her cool. Smile. Act as if nothing was wrong—at least nothing that a polite conversation couldn't fix. Drawing in a deep breath, she turned to him. "I have wine, coffee and tea. What can I get you?"

He truly was handsome. Not flashy, not a pretty boy. No, his looks leaned more toward the rugged side. But it was clear he was one of those guys who'd be as comfortable wearing a tux as he was wearing a tool belt. It didn't hurt that she found his thick eyebrows over his striking eyes very sexy. Her gaze kept floating back down to his lips, though. They were both masculine and lush. A wonderful combination. And now, they were moving.

"If it's no trouble, coffee would be great."

She turned away quickly, not sure if she'd been caught staring. "No trouble at all. Have you been here before?"

"No, I've been working on a job for the mayor."

"Ah." She smiled at the way he'd worked in that little tidbit. Was she supposed to be impressed? She worked with heads of nations on a regular basis. He'd have to try harder.

"But I think you've met my brothers." Tony had followed her to the kitchen, which consisted of a hot plate, small fridge, microwave, coffeemaker and sink. The area was a bit tight and she hadn't expected him to move in this close. Just near enough to make her pulse quicken.

Which simply wouldn't do.

"Yes, of course, Luca and…" She drew a blank. "Forgive me. I don't remember your other brother's name…"

"Dom," Tony said, lips twitching.

"Ah, right." She couldn't imagine what he found so amusing. "Dom," she said. "But it was your father with whom I had discussed the changes to my original contract."

Something flickered and died in Tony Paladino's eyes before she had a chance to interpret it, which was odd, because she could read most people in seconds.

"I understand," he said slowly, with a fair dollop of condescension.

That had to stop, as well.

"Look, I know my father is the best in the business, but he trained me from the time I could hold a wrench.

I'm not just taking over the work, but our commitment to excellence. If there was a misunderstanding we'll fix it."

Giving him a once-over she wasn't shy about, Catherine couldn't decide if she believed him or if she *wanted* to believe him. The company did have a good reputation. And while she didn't think they meant to scam her, they were most likely booked up to their eyeballs and couldn't afford the extra time for the restoration. Tearing down something and then slapping something else back up was quicker, easier and cheaper.

She opened up the coffee canister and started scooping the grounds into the pot. But her thoughts went straight back to Tony.

She guessed him to be in his early thirties, and his looks made it hard to believe he was all work and no play, but he was here and so far hadn't made any slippery moves. If she didn't count that sexy mouth of his. Well, it wasn't as if he'd picked it out of a catalog.

"From what I understand, you and my father talked about restoring as much of the original building as possible?"

That he'd cut straight to the heart of the matter startled her. She nodded, and almost lost count of the scoops. "Yes. The last time we spoke, I explained my wishes explicitly. He said he'd type up the notes and add them to the original contract, and that he'd find the right person to supervise the project. I've fallen hopelessly in love with the art deco and art nouveau of the 1930s, and I know there are remnants all over the building.

"Your father pointed out the dumbwaiter, fireplaces, crown molding, old tile patterns, the staircase and some of the door arches. And that was just a cursory look. I've seen wall plates and drawer pulls that I want to keep." She dumped in the last of the grounds and glanced back at him. "Don't get me wrong, I do want modern conveniences, of course, but if we could bring back the glamour of the bronze and silver *accoutrements*," she said, using the French pronunciation of one of her favorite words, "I'd be thrilled."

Tony looked around the room for a moment, then settled his gaze on her. He didn't speak, though, and it was becoming a little awkward, but she made it a point not to turn away first.

"All right," he said, finally, with a mysterious little smile. "I'll look for his notes, but even if I can't find them, I'll make sure you get what you want."

Catherine sighed with relief. While she was fully prepared to stand up for herself, she didn't enjoy confrontations. And if she were to be completely honest, she would've hated for Joseph or his son to disappoint her. Part of what had drawn her to this small community was the people and their culture. One she'd come to love because of her late nanny.

Belaflore Calabrese had grown up in Little Italy, and had started working for her family as a housekeeper when Catherine's parents lived in New York. She'd traveled with them to Europe and had practically raised Catherine. Belaflore had told her stories of this very house and Little Italy that Catherine still recalled with great fondness.

"The first order of business will be to take a full inventory of all the architectural details," Tony said. "We'll do that while Sal finishes up with the structural repairs. We'll see what we can find. Not everything hidden is going to be a gem." Tony frowned, took a quick look at his watch. "My father didn't give you a quote, did he?"

All her hope and faith vanished in an instant. This was where they had her all tied up in a neat little bow. They could name any price they wanted. A figure so great they would dissuade her from the project, or make a sizable profit even if they had to push back other clients.

Catherine sighed. Much as she hated the thought, it seemed the charming Tony Paladino and his father would disappoint her, after all.

2

TONY WASN'T SURE what had just happened. A few seconds ago things were warming up between him and Ms. Fox, but then she seemed to deflate.

Money. It was always about money. But she had to know that if she wanted to go all out on the restoration, it wasn't going to be cheap. "I won't be able to give you a full estimate until after you've made your decisions. My father must have mentioned this kind of restoration could be costly."

Her nod was cool. Brief. "Yes. I understand."

"Hey, I'm not trying to discourage you," Tony said, really paying attention. Wanting her to smile again, the one where her blue eyes crinkled at the corners. "You might have to do some nipping and tucking, but we'll find a way to stay within your budget."

"That's what your father told me," she said, leading him to the couch, where she sat across from him in the one uncovered chair. They were really close, their knees inches apart. "But he also told me that he would make sure to amend the contract before the renovation crew made their final decisions about plumbing and the electrical system."

She tugged her skirt down, then met Tony's gaze again. "Before you ask," she said, "I'll still want the rooms to be larger. One thing I disliked about living in Europe were all the tiny spaces. I'm five foot nine, and I felt like Alice after she swallowed the growing potion."

Tony grinned, glad to see she had her sense of humor back. He'd been right, then. She was concerned about the cost—and of course, the contract amendment—but there was nothing he could do but give her an honest appraisal. She'd probably been screwed before and was wary. He couldn't blame her.

He checked his watch again, careful to leave himself enough time to shower before he saw Rita, but there was still time to banish Catherine's worries. "There's no reason for you not to have all the space you want. Most of the remodeling we do on these old houses is combining rooms. It seems everyone wants open-concept floor plans these days, so we've gotten pretty creative about them. It's a nice surprise to have someone who wants to preserve the history of the building. I actually have someone in mind who'll be a very good fit for the restoration."

"So you won't be doing the work?"

"Not personally, no. Not now that I've taken over the office. But I've worked hands-on with all my crews, and they don't last unless they're the best."

"Taken over? What about your father?"

Tony hadn't wanted to say, but he supposed there was no secret as to what had happened. He just didn't want her to think he was second best. "Dad's had some health issues. His doctor advised him to step away from work. Some guys have all the luck, huh?"

His attempt to lighten the mood had fallen flat. Her lips were parted, but she didn't rush to speak. And again, he watched this chameleon of a woman change before his eyes. The unmistakable look of sympathy made her brow crease, her deep blue eyes darken. "I'm so sorry."

"He's fine. Really. It'll take him a while to adjust, but he's gonna be around for a long time. And he'll still make sure we don't do anything he wouldn't approve of."

Catherine leaned forward just enough that he could see a few millimeters of her creamy skin where her blouse showed off her long neck. "Please don't think I was questioning your ability."

He cleared his throat, which gave him just enough time to remember the thread of their conversation. "Nope. It never crossed my mind. The business has been in the family for generations, and we've made it this long on referrals."

"I swear I'm not making up this restoration amendment."

"Catherine." Leaning toward her, Tony nearly reached for her hand before he caught himself. "Ms. Fox—"

"Catherine is fine," she said, with an unexpectedly shy smile.

He nodded. "I didn't believe for a single second that you were lying." What had thrown him was that he'd almost made the mistake of touching her. "I meant what I said about your budget. You'll be in charge all the way. Well, the state and the city have a lot of sway here, so they'll win most of those battles."

She nodded, looked past his shoulder, then closed her eyes for a moment.

Catherine was an attractive woman. If he had to guess, he'd say she was in her late twenties. But that was based on her confidence and the way she carried herself. There was something about her face that made her look younger and, while not innocent, exactly, protected. That was why he'd almost screwed up. If he'd touched her she might have fired him on the spot and no one would have blamed her, least of all him. She was a client, for God's sake.

Shit. He'd never done anything like that before. It wasn't like him.

He needed to stop staring. It didn't help that her clothes affected him almost as much as her face. But…a black skirt that skimmed her thighs down to her kneecaps. A starched white blouse. How was that so hot? And yet…

She looked at him again, and when her fingers brushed her blond hair back, leaving trails in their wake, he was mesmerized.

The coffee gave one last loud gurgle, and she stood up so quickly he jerked back and jarred the whole couch. He took the opportunity to take a few heartening breaths before he followed her. Whatever the hell was going on with him was nuts. He didn't know her. She wasn't the kind of woman he typically went for.

Not that he was looking to go for any woman at the moment. Except for Rita. Safe, fun, comfortable Rita. That was who he should be thinking about. So, Catherine Fox? Transference. That was all this was. After tonight things would go back to normal.

Before he reached the kitchen, he checked his phone. He always turned it to Vibrate when he was with a client. So far, no messages, which was a good sign.

Joining Catherine at the counter, he bumped her shoulder as she turned, and she dropped a teaspoon.

"Sorry," he said, and bent to pick it up, but so did she and they almost collided.

"Oh."

He heard her breath stutter, a little gasp right in his ear. Instead of picking up the spoon, he steadied Catherine, his hand on her shoulder. The exact wrong move he'd just lectured himself about.

Her eyes widened and she made a sound. It was a blend of a squeal and a whimper, setting off a chain reaction that went all the way down his body.

He lowered his hand and they both straightened. He caught a glimpse of pink-splashed cheeks before she turned away. He stepped back, stealing a second to adjust himself and will his dick to knock it off.

"Cream? Sugar?" Her voice was completely controlled. Not what he'd expected.

"Uh…"

"I've also got honey, but that's more for tea."

Okay, so she wasn't quite as unruffled as she'd sounded. Coffee, though. Something to do with his mouth instead of sticking his foot in it. "Black is fine, thanks."

She got a new spoon, poured and added a packet of raw sugar to her cup. No more pink on her cheeks. Just silky smooth skin, pale and perfect.

"I'm used to living in major cities," she said, and he tried to remember the last thing they'd discussed, but came up blank.

"My last apartment was in London and that was ridiculously expensive. Worth it, though. I loved living there. I almost kept it, but that didn't seem very practical. I think New York is a better fit. There's a rhythm to the city that revs me up. I like the bustle and the sounds. The smells could be improved, but all in all, I'm glad I moved."

Europe, London, New York? He wondered what she did for a living. Something glamorous, he imagined. Definitely high up the social ladder.

They were back at the couch again, and her calm speech had relaxed him enough to gather his wits. "Listen, I have some time before my next appointment. Why don't you tell me more about what you're looking for in your overall plan?"

"Oh." She put her cup down on the end table next to her chair. "Please. Take a seat," she said, nodding at the couch. "I've collected some pictures."

"Ah, good."

"You don't mind?"

"Nope, the more I learn about what you like, the easier it will be to make your wishes come true."

She gave him a smile that made him grin back, and then she was gone. She returned quickly, holding a thick binder.

He'd moved over so she could sit beside him on the couch. Before she joined him, she twirled around before she found her coffee cup on the small table by the single chair.

"Don't worry," she said, "you don't have to look at everything. I'll just give you an idea of what I like, so that we don't have to go into a lot of detail until we catalog what I've got. Does that sound all right?"

"Excellent." Crazy, but that twirl of hers had thrown him off. He wasn't worried about her design book, just making a fool of himself. "I'm all yours."

She flipped open the cover of the binder. He immediately saw a slew of colored tabs labeled with black markers. At first, it wasn't easy to pay attention to the pictures, or the conversation, when all he really wanted was to watch her expressive face. Inhale her exotic scent. But her enthusiasm won in the end.

Her taste was eclectic—there were styles from Shaker to Asian, although he could see her heart belonged to art deco. But as she described the rooms, he could see how the styles would fit together into something uniquely hers.

There was a whole section on Little Italy alone, and while she refilled their coffee cups for the second time he looked at the pictures of the different buildings he'd either visited, studied or worked on. So much had changed in the last sixteen years. He knew that the changes had begun a long time before that, but ever since he'd started at NYU, he'd really paid attention.

Just like the rest of the city, Little Italy real estate had been hit with skyrocketing prices. Most of the people his folks had grown up with had moved to Queens, New Jersey or somewhere warm.

With each turn of the page his old appreciation for the history of his neck of the woods was reawakened. It could be an amazing place, if one landed on the right street, in the right building.

"What drew you here?" he asked. "I mean to this neighborhood. This house?"

Catherine absently ran her hand over a picture of a white bedroom suite. "I was familiar with the building. And I know how rare it is to find any single family homes here."

"You already have a buyer in mind?"

Her eyebrows drew down. "A buyer? No. This is my house. I want to live the rest of my life right here."

She wasn't flipping the place? She'd make a lot of money, especially once it was remodeled. Unfortunately, she hadn't moved into the right building at all. Not with those two neighbors on either side of her. He loved the neighborhood for the most part, but it was a tight community. It would be different if she'd settled on the fringes. As it was, the old ladies who'd kept their single family homes for generations would never make her feel welcome.

"Tony? Is there something wrong?"

He relaxed his shoulders and his attitude. "No. I'm just used to people making the old tenement buildings into either commercial properties or multiple dwellings. The prices just keep going up, so there's a lot of flipping, especially now that the old Little Italy is becoming an extension of Nolita on one end and Chinatown on the other. From what you've told me, you'd make a killing after the restoration and renovation. So I assumed."

"No. This is the house for me. I only lived in London for a year, and I knew it wasn't permanent. I've never really had a home of my own. Can't imagine a more wonderful place to start. It's why I'm being so picky about everything. I'm only sorry I haven't met any of my neighbors, or even had the chance to truly explore what's around me. But I've got time. Assuming the renovation doesn't do me in."

He smiled, but the mood that had carried them away while looking at her dream book turned sour in his gut. She might love this house, make it into a showplace of what could be done to combine the new sensibilities with the old craftsmanship. But damn, she was facing an uphill battle.

The old-timers were stuck in the past. Most of them railed against any change at all. They wanted the customs of their childhoods, the shops and open-air markets. Half the people living in these older buildings, which they'd had no compunction turning into twenty-first-century, easy-living units, still hung their laundry out their windows. But they weren't friendly to people they considered interlopers.

Should he tell her now? Make sure she understood what she was getting into?

His gaze moved down to her book of dreams and he knew he couldn't. Maybe her restoration would make the difference. It could happen. And he wouldn't be the one to take that opportunity away.

Something buzzed. A tone he didn't recognize. Catherine's cell phone. She got up to find her purse, and Tony looked at his watch once more.

His heart sank like a stone. Two hours had gone by. Two *hours*, which had felt like fifteen minutes. He pulled out his cell phone and saw four texts he'd missed. One was from Gina, the others from Rita.

He could tell by her well-chosen, very succinct words Rita was beyond pissed that he'd stood her up. No way she would talk to him even if he did call. But at least he could text her an apology. And beg for forgiveness. He knew Rita. Despite everything, she'd be willing to hook up at the next opportunity.

When Catherine walked back into the room, he understood exactly why time had flown. It was a shame he wouldn't be able to work on the restoration with her. Although it was probably for the best.

Catherine Fox was a client. An important one. This was no time to get distracted. Not when his family was counting on him. And sadly, odds were she'd be packing up soon enough. Catherine would never belong here in Little Italy.

"To making things official…boss." Luca held up his icy beer as he looked at Tony.

"Just don't take that title too seriously, but yeah," Dominic said. "To the new boss."

Tony clicked his glass to theirs and looked pointedly at Luca. "Thank you." Then he turned to face Dom. "And don't you start getting any crazy ideas in your head. Everything's going to be just like it has been. Well, there'll be a few changes, but Pop went out of his way to accommodate your website design and marketing plans, and—"

"Shut up," Dom said. "I'm a Paladino, too. I'm not about to neglect my duties. Chill."

Their waitress arrived with their dinners, and as she served them, Tony gave his youngest brother a hard look. Dom wouldn't do anything too crazy. All the kid wanted was to test out his natural gifts. He was a hell of a charmer, could sell almost anything to virtually anyone. Dom didn't want to stay in the neighborhood, Tony knew, and he would do everything in his power to make sure the kid could fly the coop. Eventually. When things were a little more stable, and after Dom finished getting his master's degree in marketing.

Tony got busy fixing his baked potato and shifted his attention to Luca. He had dreams, too. He'd make a hell of an architect once he went back to finish his apprenticeship. Their dad's poor health had temporarily turned everyone's life upside down.

"So," Luca said, "what did you think of Catherine Fox's newfound love of restoration?"

It had been a couple days since he'd met with Catherine and he'd thought about that visit far too often. "I think she'll make the place a stunner."

"Dad said she wanted to restore everything she could get her hands on," Dom said. "If this plan of hers comes together, she'll make a fortune flipping that house."

"That's the thing," Tony said, as he cut into his steak. "She doesn't want to sell it. She wants to live there. Permanently."

Luca put down his almost empty beer. "Seriously? She's got blond hair and blue eyes. I know some Italians do, but I got the impression she's *medigan*. And she wants to settle *there*?"

Tony shook his head. "I thought about saying something before she gets too invested. She's got the Masucci clan on one side and Pia Soriano on the other. Those old ladies are so goddamned determined to keep out anyone who isn't certified Italian, it's a crime."

"I don't think we have any room to throw stones," Luca said. "Isn't that what the Paladino Trust is all about?"

"Yeah, but we're trying to do exactly what Catherine's doing. Preserve what was already there. And you have to admit, Little Italy is a far cry from what it was. If she'd bought a place a couple blocks over, she'd have been fine, but—"

"Maybe she does have some Italian in her." Dom signaled the waitress with a nod and one of his guaranteed-to-dazzle smiles.

Tony shrugged. "I'm willing to be surprised."

"Even if she's not, you shouldn't tell her a damn thing until the job is done. *Capice?*"

"Ah, you're such a cynic, Dominic. Why is that?"

"Because I live in a family of saps. Someone has to have a level head."

Both Tony and Luca burst out laughing.

"What?"

"Sell that to someone who doesn't know you," Luca said. "Tony, I can go back and give the house another look if you want."

"That's okay," he said. "I've got it covered. Besides, I'm waiting for George to call me back."

"He'd do a good job. But he's booked for weeks." Luca shrugged. "If you want I can—"

"I got it."

Luca was staring and not eating. "What's going on?"

"Nothing." Tony stared back at his brother. He swore to God, sometimes he wished he had sisters instead. "What?"

"Why are you... You like her."

"Yeah." Tony switched his focus to eating his over-cooked broccoli. "I like her. She's nice."

Dom turned away from the waitress, who was already making eyes at him. "So if she's not Italian, maybe she wants a little Italian in her, huh?"

"Nice," Tony said. "Real nice. You'd better start going to Mass with Nonna. You'll never finish confessing your sins if you live to be a hundred."

Both his brothers laughed, and then still looking at Dom, Tony added, "By the way, she remembered Luca's name but she couldn't remember yours."

Luca elbowed his younger brother. "Must be losing your touch, hotshot."

Dom's look of disbelief was almost comical.

Luca said, "By the way, how's Rita?"

Tony rolled his eyes. "Look, Catherine's interesting, okay?"

"I'd changed the subject already," Luca said, grinning. "But if you want to talk about Catherine, then yeah, she's very attractive, in her own way. But a little aloof. You know what I mean?"

"No, actually, I don't. She's very—"

Luca smiled at him.

"Shut up and eat your fish."

Dom took a bite of his T-bone, but still said, "Hell, she's got to be loaded to buy that house and do all those renovations. Maybe she's an heiress or something."

"Dad mentioned she works at the UN," Luca said. "As an interpreter or something like that."

Tony shrugged, ready to drop the topic of Catherine Fox. Yeah, he'd thought a lot about her in the last couple days. And she wasn't off-putting or anything like that. He could see why someone might get the wrong impression, but only because of the way she moved. She stood and sat like a ballet dancer, or a model or something. Smooth as silk.

He couldn't get over that damn little twirl she'd done when she'd forgotten her coffee cup. It wasn't exactly stroke material, but it kept playing in his head, like an ear worm, but one he could see.

Which was stupid. He couldn't afford to give her so much real estate. He had a company to run now. And Dom was right about her having enough capital to become a very profitable client. There was still time to take Luca up on his offer to take over until George was free.

But Tony knew damn well he wasn't going to do the sensible thing.

3

FINALLY, THE ELECTRICIAN was gone. He'd been the last of the day crew to leave. She knew Sal's team was working very hard to give her the house she wanted, but today that had meant moving wiring that displaced her temporary kitchen and living room. After a good deal of consideration, she'd decided not to move into a hotel until the restoration was done.

Although she was beginning to doubt it would ever start, let alone finish.

Tony had sent her the contract amendment, worded so that she'd have an out if the cost became too high. Along with it was a note assuring her that he was following through with hiring a restoration expert, but the one he had in mind might not be available for a couple weeks. She'd hoped Tony would've delivered the envelope in person, but she had something more important to consider. Whether to wait and put the renovation on hold if his man was unavailable? Or settle for second best?

All she needed for this first phase was someone who understood the history and architecture of the 1920s and '30s. Her goal was to make sure she caught everything in the inventory of objects to restore. Any moment now,

Fred, a man Tony was sending, would arrive to excavate while she cataloged his findings. She'd already changed into her casual clothes and was impatient to find out what treasures lay in wait.

The bell rang when she was halfway down the stairs. She hurried the rest of the way down and swung open the door.

Tony.

He wasn't supposed to be here.

And yet there he was, making her blush, somehow forcing her head to dip so she had to look at him through her eyelashes. As if she were a schoolgirl. Actually, she'd been way too sensible in her teens for that kind of display.

She stopped that nonsense in the next heartbeat. "Tony," she said, making it almost a question, but in truth, it was a challenge.

"Hey. I hope this is all right. Me, instead of Fred. I can assure you that I know what I'm doing."

"No. I mean, yes. It's fine," she said, carefully keeping her response neutral. "Of course." She stepped back. "Please, come in."

He stood close after she shut the door. It would have been polite for her to back away, but once she caught the scent of something woodsy and masculine she didn't want to move. Odd, since she was very protective of her personal space. Tony just looked too damned good in his chambray shirt and a pair of worn jeans.

If she'd known he was coming, she would have put on something other than the old khakis and knit shirt she'd thrown on. She certainly would have put on a little more makeup. Done something more flattering to her hair—

Good Lord, what was happening to her?

"Turns out George and Fred are both tied up with other

projects. We really can't afford to wait. The domino effect could put us too far behind."

She smiled. "That's not what I've been led to believe about contractors. Aren't they legendary for making people wait?"

"Not Paladino & Sons. Well, okay, sometimes delays happen, but we try to give realistic estimates, and let our customers know ahead of time if there might be a prob—" His eyes warmed with humor. "You were joking."

She nodded, caught by the way he was staring at her. No noticeable blinking. Relaxed grin. His hand had recently pushed back his dark hair, and, oh, God, she'd seen that exact same look in dozens of romantic films. "It's nice to see you again," she said, thankful she'd been trained from birth to keep everything she felt to herself. "May I get you anything? Coffee? Wine?"

He shook his head, but his gaze didn't budge.

"It's a very nice cabernet from a great vineyard in Italy."

"Well, as good as that sounds, I am here to work."

Catherine felt the heat creeping up her neck. "Of course," she said, turning away. "I wasn't thinking."

"But as long as the vineyard's in Italy... I wouldn't turn down a glass after we've finished for the evening."

"The offer stands." Leading him upstairs, she allowed herself a foolish grin, but kept her pace steady. Deciding not to dwell on the the fact that he was probably checking out her ass, she said, "I've done a little sleuthing on my own," she said. "I'd planned on getting a good chunk of the inventory done by myself, but I was foiled by the mystery of what's hiding underneath the paint on the fireplace mantel." She pointed to the south wall.

Tony frowned. "Did you try to remove any paint?"

"Not really. I read that there was a good chance the paint had lead in it. I didn't have the right safety gear, which I've since taken care of. But I did scrape a bit. It looks like it'll be worth the work, at least to see if it's cast iron."

"That's great. Good thinking." He pulled out his cell phone. "Are you interested in doing some of the restoration work yourself?"

"I am. Nothing too taxing. I've never done anything like it. I'm not all that good with my hands, but it would be nice to know I had a small part."

Tony met her gaze, and from where she was standing, he looked pleased. Although it could have been the light.

Then, he went right back to typing something on his phone.

"Are you texting Fred or George?"

"No. I've got an app where I keep all my notes and plans. I've already put in the basic layout of the house, so I'll be able to mark it up as we find pieces we want to investigate."

Tony pulled out a Swiss Army knife from his back pocket, went to the fireplace and crouched by the side of the unit. Catherine crouched next to him, watching what he did. The first thing she noticed was he scraped a lot harder than she had.

His next move was to cut the linoleum that butted up against the painted surround. A moment later, he found something that made his face light up.

"What is it?"

"Tile. I can't promise all of it will be intact, but all we really need is one."

"You can get it duplicated?"

"Again, it's costly, but yes, we can."

"Okay, one thing you should know. You don't have to

be concerned with the budget. While I appreciate your warnings, I think it will make things easier for both of us if we just wait until the full estimate is complete. Then I'll make my choices. Okay?"

He nodded as he stood up, and once again they were standing too close for politeness's sake. It wouldn't have been a problem if they were in Tokyo. But New Yorkers needed at least a thousand square feet of personal space to be truly comfortable. No, this was Manila close.

"You'll have to show me your safety gear. I'll let you know if everything comes up to code," he said, those damnable dark eyes capturing her own once more.

The sentence was benign, the look wasn't. Seconds ticked by as heat circled through her while he stared. It grew stronger when he let out a breath that reached her, minty fresh. Maybe this whole thing was all about scent, but then why had the swirling heat started the second she'd opened the front door?

None of this was okay. It was bad enough she couldn't read him, but now she couldn't even make sense of herself.

After he inhaled—something that should have given her a hundred clues—he stepped back. Walked to the other side of the room to inspect the crown molding.

Great. Now she was making him uncomfortable.

Catherine shook herself out of her trance. "Would it bother you if I had a glass of wine?"

"Not at all."

She made sure she downed half a glass before she rejoined him. She also promised herself that she would focus on learning about her new home, not her general contractor.

It was an education, walking through each room with him. He welcomed her questions, even though she knew she was going a bit overboard. But with each move, he stepped in closer. First, just their shoulders touched. A brush. Insignificant, but for how aware of it she was. The rooms were small. The physical contact would have happened between any two adults. But by the time they hit the downstairs powder room they squeezed into the tight space as if they were old hands at this touching business.

"I'm pretty sure that if you want to enlarge this bathroom we can keep to the original aesthetic," Tony said, his voice a couple notches above a whisper. "But I need to know more about the plumbing before we can make any decisions."

"I don't mind this bathroom being small, if it allows me to open up the living and dining rooms."

Tony continued to look directly into her eyes. His lips parted as if he was going to say something. But he didn't, and it was all she could do not to lean those few inches forward. Unlock his words with a touch of her tongue.

A honking horn out on the street brought her back to reality and she gained control quickly and moved out of the powder room. "It's the bathroom upstairs that has me worried."

He added a few more notes to his app before they climbed back up the old staircase. He went to the fireplace and picked up her wineglass. "That covers the big things," he said. "But there are lots of details that we haven't cataloged." His gaze skated over the mess, where before there had at least been chairs. Then he took a sip.

She cleared her throat, not minding that he'd taken a sip of her wine, but worried he'd feel embarrassed. "Sorry about the accommodations. The only place I seem to have left for company is the staircase or my bedroom."

Tony blinked at the wineglass, a brief look of shock on his face. "Uh, it's no problem," he said. He put the glass back on the mantel, a slight blush warming his cheeks. "Sorry about that. Look, I've got something I have to do tomorrow evening, and I'm sure you'll want some peace and quiet on Sunday, but I could come back Monday. After the others have left."

"You?"

"Or Fred," he said, taking half a step back.

"No, that's… While I've got you here, there are a few more pictures I wanted you to see, if you have time…"

"I've got a few minutes."

She went first to the kitchen area and poured him a glass of his own. Then she handed it to him as she segued into her bedroom. Her queen mattress barely fit in the space, but at least they could sit side by side. She picked up her binder, which was lying atop a box of hard-backed books.

Tony stood at the door.

"Come. Sit," she said, patting the bed. It wasn't a problem. They'd have the whole binder between them. "I know we're trying to save as much of the old as we can, but when we were looking at the staircase, I was underwhelmed."

As they discussed alternatives, Catherine reminded herself it would be wise to remember that Tony wasn't part of her dreams for this house. Even if the spark she felt was reciprocated, which seemed unlikely. She'd never been attracted to a man like Tony before, and she had no idea if it was against any rules for them to have anything but a working relationship.

"There's a metalwork artist in Connecticut that does meticulous work on railings and more. In fact, I planned on asking him to come down and go over the fireplaces, anyway."

"Perfect," she said, as her stomach rumbled so loudly it made him choke back a laugh.

"Sorry," she said. "I haven't had dinner. I'm probably going to order something in. Would you like to join me?"

His head tilted about five degrees to the right, and his gaze moved from hers to his lower arm, where, she realized, she was touching him.

"That's very nice of you, but—"

She moved her hand away with lightning speed. "Since I seem to be monopolizing your time I figured I should at least offer..."

"No problem," Tony nodded, staring just past her left ear.

She stood up, aware he'd know what an arm touch meant. "I've been wanting some decent Chinese, is all. No big deal."

"There's a great place not too far from here."

Her grin must have looked ridiculous. Jesus. Seconds after she'd just finished thinking he was off-limits. And probably married. Not all men wore wedding rings. Especially those who did construction work. "Really? I don't know much about the local hotspots. Too much work and not enough time for exploring."

"I can help out with that," he said, standing up himself. Taking a step closer to her. "At least steer you away from some dubious choices."

She blinked at him. Was he this helpful to all his clients? If so, that would explain why his company had such a great reputation.

He did something on his cell phone, and then handed it to her. On the screen was a menu for a Szechuan restaurant at an address she wasn't familiar with.

"They're a little slow on the delivery, but they're worth

it. I've never had a bad meal from them. I think you'll
be pleased."

"So, was that a no to joining me?"

"Don't think I can."

"Okay, but the thing I wanted to talk to you about. It's
kind of a big deal."

"Shoot."

"I'm considering a rooftop garden. A decent-sized one,
maybe one some of the neighbors could use, as well." She
flipped to the back pages and handed him the binder.
While he glanced at the sample gardens, she grabbed
her iPhone off her dresser and called the restaurant. Her
order was large, but that was what she got for waiting
until she was this hungry.

Or Tony could change his mind. No, she had to stop
that sort of thinking.

By the time she'd finished giving her address, Tony
was seated again, and watching her, a slight smile tug-
ging at his mouth.

"What?"

"You must really like Chinese food."

"I do." She laughed. "I even like it for breakfast."

His brows rose. "Good thing."

"Don't knock it until you try it."

"Hey, I'm the same way. I'll eat the stuff any time
of the day—" He'd been about to say more but stopped
himself.

She'd wager anything she'd surprised him. Which
wasn't a bad thing.

Not a bad thing at all.

With her own secret smile, she sat down again. Too
late, she realized it might've been better for her to have
remained standing. They weren't sitting indecently close
or anything—she'd left some space between them—but

she could feel the warmth of his body pulling at her, distracting her from the point of the conversation.

She cleared her throat. "I volunteer at the community gardens at the UN," she said, relieved her voice sounded normal. "Where I work. Obviously, this wouldn't be as large, but my roof is flat and I'm pretty sure there's room enough for what I have in mind. What I don't know is if it's possible."

"That's…a big job. A very… There's a lot to consider. We've done a few, all on restaurant rooftops."

"I know. I saw on your website."

He hesitated again and got that inscrutable look on his face. "There are so many things that all have to work for it to be possible. The weight of a garden can be tremendous. We'd need to call in a structural engineer to begin with. Then there are permits, including using a crane on a street that isn't very wide."

"I understand. But I'd like to find out if it's possible before I fall too far in love with the idea."

"I'll look into it."

Something was clearly bothering him. She didn't think she should ask. It was just as likely to be her imagination. But when he abruptly got to his feet, she knew it wasn't.

"But now, I really do have to leave."

Disappointed, Catherine accompanied him downstairs, and when she opened the front door, there was a kid sitting on the bottom step of her stoop. She couldn't imagine what he was doing there.

He jumped to his feet and looked at Tony. "Hey, Mr. Paladino. Nonna wants you to come over. She's got something wrong with—" his face, pale under the unflattering outdoor light, scrunched with thought "—something in the kitchen."

Tony frowned. "When did your grandma send you over? It's almost seven o'clock."

The kid, who looked to be around ten, shrugged. "I dunno. She and my mom were arguing about something. Then I was supposed to come here. Wait to catch you before you went home."

Tony turned to Catherine. "Sorry. This is Ricky Alberti. His grandmother is your neighbor."

She smiled at the boy. "Nice to meet you."

When Tony stepped outside, his frown looked even more doleful in the bad light. "You tell your grandma that she should call Gina for an appointment. No. Have her call me. I'll tell her myself."

Ricky shrugged again. "'Kay." Then he was off like a shot.

"I'm sorry about that," Tony said, sounding irritated despite the easy smile. "He shouldn't have been hanging around your stoop."

"It's no problem. I find it kind of charming, actually. The sign of a tight neighborhood."

The brief glance toward the neighbor's house indicated he didn't agree. Huh. "Well, I'm not thrilled at being at everyone's beck and call. Anyway, I'll be going now." He took two steps down before turning to her again. "Hope you like the dumplings. They're my favorite."

Grateful the tension had vanished, she almost asked him to stay and have some of hers, but she stopped herself just in time. "Good night, Tony. Thank you. For tonight."

He smiled, nodded, but didn't look at her again. He just hurried away.

She closed the door, and wished very hard that he'd forgotten something. His cell phone. A jacket. To kiss her.

4

By Monday afternoon, Tony had finished transferring what he needed to make his father's old office feel like his own. He'd also gotten more comfortable with being the boss, although there were a few decisions he wished his father could have made.

He heard a low voice in the reception area, one he'd recognize in a blackout. Well, at least the old man had lasted almost a whole week without coming to check up on his empire.

Tony was delighted to see that his mom had come, too, and that Joe was wearing a Hawaiian-print shirt, one he was allowed to wear only on vacations. They were both chatting with Gina as if their separation had been years instead of days. Tony joined them, giving his mother a kiss on the cheek. "Worried the place was falling apart?"

Joe gave him a scowl. "You think I don't trust you? I trust you. The real question is do you trust you?"

"I'm working on it, Pop. I don't know if I'll ever figure out how you kept Luca and Dom in line."

His mother frowned, although he knew the look was more for effect than anything. "All three of you were no picnic, believe me."

"I know." Tony grinned. "Honestly, though, they've both been fine. Luca, a little finer than Dominic. You know how he is. The kid thinks he's Sinatra or something, and he's tone deaf."

"Sinatra was from Jersey," Gina said. "Dom wants to be the king of Little Italy."

"It's a small kingdom." Tony walked over to the whiteboard without really looking at it. "Getting smaller by the day."

"We're not going to talk about work," his mother said. Theresa was really the boss of the family, and everyone knew that. She didn't mind leaving the details to her brood, but anything big was Ma's domain.

"All right," Tony said. "Is this a stopover visit on your way to rehab?"

Joseph cursed in Italian the same second Tony's mother said, "Yes. This stubborn mule of a husband thinks he's wasting his time. You'd think the second heart attack would have gotten through his thick head."

It actually felt good, hearing the two of them bicker. Like home.

Tony had to take a phone call, so he went to his office. It was Dave, the metalworker he'd called about Catherine's staircase and fireplaces. Tony gave him some preliminary measurements and Catherine's number.

Just as he ended the call, he realized his father had entered the room. He was looking at all the things Tony had changed. Slowly. Making a mental tally. The expression on his face broke Tony's heart. Made him wish he'd never changed anything at all.

"It's good," Joe said. "You taking over."

"It's necessary," Tony told him, walking around the desk to sit on the front corner to free up his pop's old chair. "We need you to stick around as our dad way more than we need you to run this place."

"I know the reasons. There's just so damn many hours in the day. Even with three meals and a visit to the torture room, I've still got too much empty space."

"Ma hasn't put you to work?"

"Stupid things, sure. A real project, like painting that spare room? She thinks I'll die on her Persian carpet."

"Have you tried going to the park like we talked about?"

"I don't like the way they changed the park. Too many strangers and kids."

"They're only strangers until you talk to them. You like chess. They play chess."

"I like playing with people I know."

"And what do you mean you don't like kids? That's not true."

"I want grandkids," Joe grumbled. "Not strangers' kids. You and Angie should've had two bambinos by now, instead of getting divorced."

Tony's insides coiled into a knot. "Come on, Pop, we're not going to talk about that."

Joe shrugged. "So, I hear you're working personally with Catherine Fox."

"How do you know that?"

"I got ears that work. She's got big pockets, that one. Very deep. She has some crazy ideas, but they're not so crazy if you think about them."

"You mean the restoration?"

"The value of the house will go up, you know that. Along with making the upgrades."

"She wants a rooftop garden."

Joe's eyes widened. "No kidding."

"What's worse? She wants to live there. Full-time."

Joe moved across the room and settled into his old black chair.

Tony smiled to himself and took one of the guest chairs.

"She could make a fortune selling that place. When she gets done with it, garden or no, it'll be a jewel on that street."

"I know. But she doesn't want to go."

"With those old ladies she's got for neighbors? She'll want to."

Tony knew more about those two than he'd like. They'd both called him in the last couple days. Asked every question in the book about Catherine. He'd cut them off, refused to discuss his client with them. When all he'd wanted to do was tell them both where to go. But he was his mother's son, so he'd been nice…ish.

Speaking of his mother, she walked in right at that moment and made her famous whimper of exasperation while throwing her hands up in the air. As if the world itself was ending.

She slapped Tony's shoulder. "You just let him take over? The first time we come to visit you start talking business?"

Shaking his head, Tony held back a smile.

"What business?" his father said, gesturing expansively. "I'm sitting in my old chair. Is that a crime?"

She put her hands on her hips and glared at him.

"Fine. A little about business, but I was just making an observation. That's not work."

"Is that true, Tony?"

"That's true."

"Why am I listening to you?" she asked. "You're your father's son. We have to leave now, but next time I see you, Anthony Paladino, I expect you to be more careful with your father. He's not a healthy man."

She was right, although Tony couldn't see cutting him off from the business cold turkey. But he'd try to make both his parents happy. Which hadn't been possible in thirty-three years, so why he should keep trying was anyone's guess.

"Try the park again," Tony said, as they were leaving. "Play some chess."

"And you…go make me some grandkids."

"Stop it." His mother bumped his dad's shoulder. "What's the matter with you? He's divorced." She glanced at Tony and shook her head. "Don't listen to him. Angie was a nice girl, but she was too modern."

He didn't say a word. Angie was from the neighborhood. His parents had known her parents for years. She wasn't a great cook, but that meant she wasn't competition for the crown of Tony's Favorite, which actually made his mother like Angie even more. She was exactly the kind of girl everyone had imagined for him, but the marriage hadn't worked out. At least they'd parted amicably.

When his folks had left, he had to make two more phone calls, and then pay a visit to a new customer in Chinatown.

After that, he knew exactly where he was going.

Exactly where he shouldn't.

Where he couldn't wait to go.

THE LINE INTO Ferrara's bakery was long, but it seemed to be moving pretty quickly. Catherine had been there several times, and loved their pastries, but this evening she was buying for two. Tony was coming over.

They were going to take a look at her rooftop. Sal was still in charge of the renovations, but Tony had decided to supervise the restoration and the garden project. He'd told her he'd be there around six thirty, after dinner with his parents. She hoped he hadn't had any dessert.

The line moved again, this time allowing her a great view of the glass display case. Everything there looked wonderful, but she'd already decided what she'd get for this evening: three different pastries she could vouch for personally. He was bound to like at least one of them.

Two women a few people in front of her caught her attention because they were speaking in Italian. She thought one of them might be her neighbor. Catherine had seen the woman standing on her front stoop the other day. It was obvious they hadn't noticed her because they didn't bother to lower their voices, or consider that she might speak Italian.

"That one has workers all day, making so much noise I'm not getting a bit of work done."

She strained to hear the other woman's response but couldn't.

"For all I know," her neighbor went on, "she's turning that beautiful place into apartments."

The conversation stopped when the person in front of them left.

Catherine watched them place their orders with the woman behind the counter, torn between wishing she'd heard more and glad she hadn't. Of course they were upset with the noise. And she hated for anyone to think she would turn the beautiful home into apartments, but now wasn't the time to clear the air.

The women paid and left without any sign they'd noticed her. Thank goodness. Once the construction was over, she figured things would all work out.

"Great minds really do think alike."

Catherine spun around at Tony's voice. His smile was broad, his eyes crinkling at the edges.

"I was going to pick up dessert. For us," she said. "For later."

"My thoughts exactly."

"Hmm," she said, feeling awkward and pleased at the same time. Why she should feel tongue-tied around Tony when she could face off with Vladimir Putin, she had no idea. "Well, maybe it's a good thing you're here. I won't have to guess what you might like."

"What were you going to get?"

She shifted a bit to her left so he could move in closer, letting people pass him more easily. "No fair. I asked you first."

"Technically, you didn't ask, but it would be rude for me to point that out."

"Wouldn't want to be rude."

Tony smiled. "There aren't many things here I don't like. But their cannoli are very good." He leaned closer, so close that his breath tickled her ear. "Better than my mother's, to be honest, but I would never tell her that. Ever. In fact, I need you to swear that you won't ever speak of it again."

Catherine crossed her heart, which remained inconveniently fluttery.

"Have you been here before?" he asked.

"Yes. Too often. I have a problem with pastries. I like them too much."

"As much as Chinese food?"

Letting out a laugh, she narrowed her eyes at him. "You don't need to speak of that again, either."

"Guess we're even," he said with a wink.

She had no idea what to do with that. It wasn't a flirty wink; at least she didn't think so. Not many men had winked at her before. She kind of liked it. Her heart sure was getting a workout, though.

Luckily, the line moved again, putting them face-to-face with the counter girl. "Four cannoli," Catherine said as quickly as possible, anxious to make this her treat, not his. "Two lobster tails and two panfortes."

While she'd been faster on the draw with the order, Tony already had his wallet out. "Put that away," she said. "You're the one helping me out when you don't have to."

"I'm an Italian man in a bakery where they know me. You want everyone in town to talk about how I let you pay for my dessert?"

"Well, that's incredibly chauvinistic. Please tell me you don't mean it."

His shrug said an awful lot.

"I lived in Italy," she said, "and no one was that ridiculous."

"I think you'll find there are many anachronisms in our little village. We're losing so much territory to the soaring encroachment from every angle, I think the old-timers are doing their best to keep everything old-fashioned even when it doesn't make a damn bit of difference."

"Fine," Catherine said, when he pulled out some bills. She thought briefly about mentioning what she'd overheard, but dismissed the idea. "You buy them this time. But just the once."

"I'll even carry the box," he said.

When the girl came back with his change, she barely looked at Tony. Instead, she was checking out Catherine as if there'd be a test. It didn't surprise her at all when the young woman said, "See you later, Tony. And tell that brother of yours I saved him a slice of cheesecake."

"Sorry," Tony said, touching the back of Catherine's blazer with his broad hand, steering her toward the exit. "I doubt I'll see Dom anytime soon."

"Maybe she meant Luca."

Tony laughed. "Nope. Dom. Guaranteed."

Once they were on the street, it wasn't a long walk to her house, and the lowering sun made everything look golden and beautiful. She thought again about how he'd so recently taken over the business from his father, and yet, he kept showing up after hours. "You do know I can wait for Fred or George," she said. "The list of things to be restored is daunting and I'm positive you have a great deal on your plate."

"I don't mind," he said. "It's been good for me to keep my hand in the game. I'd been doing more of the managing before my father finally retired. It's all about delegating." He slowed to a stop. "Would you mind a small detour? I know Sal's going to be working with you on your front stoop, but there are two you might like to see. Both designed by the metalworker I told you about."

"I'd love to see them."

They turned at the next corner, and she realized that while she'd found places like the bakery and the dry cleaners, she really hadn't spent any time at all exploring the side streets. Most of the buildings were old remodeled tenements. Five, six, even seven stories high. Almost every ground and basement floor was occupied by a retail business, everything from restaurants to art galleries to delis.

She'd given thought to renting out her own basement floor space. The last owners, Belaflore's family, had run a popular resale clothing shop. Catherine had bought some things there before she'd purchased the building. One of her favorite dresses, in fact. There was still time to change her mind about using the entire two-story building with the bonus basement as her home. If she did decide to rent out the lower level, it would be only to help her fit in more with the community. But she doubted she would. She didn't need the money, which was pure luck, having been born to a wealthy family, but more important, she wanted enough space to have children someday. Space was an extraordinary luxury in Manhattan, and wouldn't it be something to pass down a family home like hers?

Her slice of Lafayette was an anomaly. But one she wanted to preserve.

"Hey, Tony."

They turned to a portly man standing in the doorway of an electronics store. He was smiling as he gave Catherine a once-over.

"Hey, Pete," Tony said.

"How's your old man?"

"Hanging in there. Driving my mom crazy."

"Tell him he still needs to come to the merchants' meetings. No excuses."

"I will, Pete. Thanks." Tony kept walking, although he didn't seem to be in any rush to move on. "Be warned," he said, leaning closer to her so he could be heard above the street traffic. "That's going to happen a lot."

"I'd already figured out you were very popular among the citizenry."

"If by popular you mean everyone wants to know my business, then yeah."

"Does your business include you walking down the street with me? With your hand on the small of my back?"

His hand disappeared the next second. "Damn. Sorry."

"I didn't say I minded."

He looked at her, a little puzzled. "It's not so simple. None of these goombahs will stop to think you might be a client. They'll jump the gun and assume we're a couple. So if, you know, you're engaged or anything..."

"That would be bad."

"It would."

"Good thing I'm not, then."

He turned to look across the street just when she'd wanted to see his expression. Wouldn't her mother be surprised at her brazen reply. Even in London she'd probably have been more circumspect. Maybe this was part of her becoming a New Yorker. Or maybe it just had to do with the man. He made her feel bolder, whether it was getting her hands dirty polishing old sconces, or buying pastry in the hopes he'd stay a little longer this time.

Of course, her mother would be appalled by all of it, but her mother would have been much happier if she'd been born in the Victorian age. Her father was more progressive...sort of. Then again, the man wore a suit, tie and waistcoat to work every day, and to dinner, even.

"See that," Tony said, pointing to a stoop that had a gorgeous railing alongside its five steps. The railing matched a lantern that was so much more elegant than the utilitarian light fixture she had now.

"May I get a closer look?"

"Sure."

At first she thought he was going to take her hand, but after checking for traffic, he simply gestured for them to cross.

"Oh, this is lovely," she said, running her hand over the intricate work, the curlicues that weren't at all overdone, just beautiful.

"Tony Paladino. You haven't been by in a hundred years." A tall trim woman with short brown hair stood in the doorway of a store next door.

"I don't think it's been quite that long, Mrs. Collette. But it's nice to see you."

"How is your father?"

"Doing better, thank you."

"Good to hear it." She eyed Catherine, though not in a rude manner. "And who's your friend?"

"Catherine Fox, this is Mrs. Collette. I think you'll like her store. There are quite a few antiques that could fit in well with your renovations."

Catherine had already spotted a console table near the door that appealed to her...before she'd been distracted by Tony's clever way of saying-without-saying she was a client. She smiled at Mrs. Collette. "I'd love to come back when I have enough time to really explore. Are you open on the weekend?"

"Saturday. You come back then. If you like real antiques, that is. Not like that *avanzo* Caliguiri sells."

"I'll be here the first Saturday I can manage. Thank you."

"My pleasure. And Tony, I don't think we've spoken since you and Angie... I was sorry about that. She's a nice girl. I thought you two were made for each other."

"Yeah, well, take care, Mrs. Collette," Tony said, as he moved the two of them forward. "The second stoop is the next block over. Then what do you say we head to your place? These pastries are calling my name."

Catherine was curious about Angie, but she would never ask him. "Absolutely."

He put his hand on her back as they crossed the street, but dropped it again as soon as they were on the sidewalk. He wasn't kidding around about this discretion business, although she'd liked the protective touch even if it was just a guy thing. Three other people asked about Tony's father, and Tony was courteous to each one, despite the fact that they barely slowed to talk.

The second stoop was also gorgeous, and it made her very excited about the possibilities for her home. But by the time she opened her front door, she was thinking more about the evening that lay ahead than the prospects for her stoop.

"I'm going to make coffee," she said. "And while we wait, why don't we go up to the roof? You can take a look at the setup and I'll talk you through my initial plans."

"I think that's a great idea."

"Great, huh?"

"Well…" His voice dipped as his mouth curved into a heart-stopping smile. "I figure anything that ends in cannoli is bound to be something special."

God, she hoped that was innuendo.

The idea that she didn't know made her nervous, but maybe not being able to read Tony was part of the thrill?

It didn't take long to get their coffee started, and then they went through the attic exit to the rooftop.

The sun had set, but the lights she turned on illuminated the space adequately for the purpose. "I'm thinking six raised beds," she said, waving her hand across the breadth of the roof. "We'll have to do something about that horrendous air-conditioning unit, but that shouldn't be too challenging. And I'd like to have some hedges and a few good, sturdy conifers that will make winter more appealing. A pergola perhaps, over a deck where people could sit, eat, enjoy the view, the change of seasons. And then I was—"

Her words froze as Tony took her by the arms and turned her around to face him. She had the advantage of the light, and she thought, for a moment, that the look in his eyes was want.

He pulled her close, opened his mouth to speak, but no words came. Instead, his right thumb brushed her cheekbone as his gaze swept across her face. A faint smile lifted the corners of his lips. It vanished just as quickly, as if he'd come to his senses or something equally disappointing.

And then he kissed her.

Kissed her as if he'd wanted to for ages.

She'd been unprepared, even though the brush across her cheek had been a substantial clue. Her response, though, was slow. She simply let him go on kissing her, trying and failing to make sense of anything but the way he moved his mouth. Wider, tighter, gentler.

A groan escaped and she parted her lips, kissed him back, touched his side with her hand before grabbing on to his shirt.

When he pulled back, he studied her expression, his gaze moving rapidly. When she smiled, she felt him relax before he stole her breath with another kiss.

Somewhere, a door slammed. The sound didn't come from her roof, but close. Tony froze as if it had been a gunshot, and he backed away from her as quickly as he could. "Jesus, I'm sorry." He shook his head. "The plans for the garden are great," he said, moving toward the door. "I'll write it all down before I call the designer I have in mind. I really am sorry."

"Tony—"

He held up a hand. "Won't happen again. I promise you."

And then he was gone.

She heard his shoes hit the first few steps of the attic stairs, then nothing.

She, on the other hand, stood there blinking. Wondering how she'd been caught so off guard, when she'd been flirting with him from the moment they'd met at the bakery. She wished she'd told him to stay. That he didn't need to be sorry. That they were supposed to have dessert downstairs.

What the hell was it about Tony Paladino that turned her knees weak and her mind to mush? He wasn't even the type of man to whom she was usually attracted. This. Him. Her. Nothing made any sense at all. But she hoped like crazy that he'd break his promise because she really wanted to kiss him again.

5

TONY HAD BEEN up at the crack of dawn. Not because of work, but because he'd been awake most of the night.

It wasn't that he'd kissed her. Well, yeah, that was part of it. But hell, he'd wanted to do that for a while. But his exit? Clumsy didn't come close. He'd acted like an idiot. Left her standing alone on her rooftop. He'd practically flown down the stairs, and when he made it to the street, he'd grabbed the first cab he saw to take him home. He didn't even live that far away, but he was afraid he'd walk in the wrong direction or take the wrong train.

Jesus.

He'd had a couple drinks first thing upon arriving at his place. Stopped himself from having several more. Oblivion would have been welcome, but the hangover would not. That kind of reckless behavior would have been borderline acceptable before he was boss, but now he had to toe the line.

Which would have been a clever thing to think about *before* he'd kissed a client.

All he'd had to do, if the situation was so desperate, was ask Luca to take over for him until George was free. Instead, he'd listened to her garden plans, of which he couldn't remember one single detail, behaved like an imbecile and fled as if he'd been set on fire.

At least the humiliation had stopped his burgeoning erection. By the time he'd climbed into the cab, he was reasonably sure he'd never get hard again.

Which turned out to be yet another stupid assumption.

Despite swearing that he would think only of Rita as he shook one off in the shower, the moment he'd touched himself, Rita hadn't crossed his mind again. Christ. And she could be coming back through town anytime.

Maybe sex with Rita was the answer.

God, wouldn't that be great, if it worked?

Although, at around three this morning, he'd found himself with his hand on his dick once again, and yeah, it was all about Catherine in that black skirt and white blouse.

At least he'd come up with a plan. Which was why, at just after one in the afternoon, he was standing outside the United Nations visitors' entrance, typing in a text.

He tried to imagine where Catherine was. What her office looked like. What she did. Luca said something about her being a translator. But Catherine hadn't said and Tony hadn't asked. So much for avoiding personal questions and staying professional. Here he was, with no idea if she was even in one of the buildings he faced. Was she in the big tower or the general assembly? Already out to lunch?

After hitting Send, he walked for a bit. Paced, actually, iPhone in hand. When he caught an older man staring at him, he stopped. Bad place to look suspicious.

His phone beeped and he opened the reply.

Hi. I'm just leaving. I'll meet you out front.

He thought about texting back, but that seemed lame. She was on her way. He hadn't asked her to lunch. Not yet. He wanted to speak to her in person. See what kind of reaction she'd have at his surprise appearance.

Maybe five minutes later, he caught sight of her. Catherine wasn't alone. Her companion was a man in a suit. Who looked like he belonged next to her. As they got closer, Tony wasn't all that crazy about the way Catherine laughed at something suit-guy had said. Shit. He might be a delegate. Clearly someone important. Elegant.

Very much in keeping with Catherine's sophistication. She always seemed to hold her back straight, her head high. Her honey-blond hair was pinned up, her blouse almost the color of her blue-gray eyes, and her pants an invitation to look slowly from her flat stomach down her long legs.

At least Tony had pulled himself together before she spotted him.

He should have called her. Her voice would have told him so much more than a text. Maybe she'd have given him a heads-up about the guy. Boyfriend? She'd told him she wasn't engaged, but that didn't mean she wasn't seeing someone.

More than likely, she was pissed at him. The stunt he'd pulled last night was unforgivable. He hoped she'd give him a chance, though. If he swore he'd keep his distance.

The thought of never kissing her again wasn't pleasant, but he pasted on a casual smile as Catherine and friend stopped right in front of him.

"What a nice surprise," she said. "Are you working in the area today?"

Huh. No introduction. "I have an appointment later, so I thought…"

Catherine turned her head to her friend. "Victor, this is my contractor, Tony Paladino. Tony, my coworker, Victor Bardon."

Oh, Victor didn't like that intro, but at least he wasn't trying to prove his manliness via a handshake.

She glanced at her companion. "I'll see you this afternoon, *oui*?"

"*Oui*. Nice to meet you, Tony," he said, showing off his French accent.

Tony had been spot on about Monsieur Bardon. Judging by the look he gave Catherine, Vic didn't want to be just her coworker. At least he didn't dawdle. He kept walking down First Avenue toward Forty-Sixth. Once he was out of earshot, Tony turned his attention to Catherine. "Were you planning on eating lunch?"

She nodded, smiling, looking as if the awkwardness of last night's kiss had never happened. "I was going to go to the house. I have some leftover tuna fish in need of eating."

"As delicious as that sounds, how would you feel about me taking you to the best pizza parlor in New York."

"The best?"

"Hands down. Also, not something I share with many. So, I'll have to invoke the no-repeating rule. I have a feeling the pizza chefs in Little Italy would object. Probably using tar and feathers."

"Wow, Little Italy really is old-fashioned. But yes, that sounds much better than my rather dull salad."

"Good. It's not too far from here." He nodded toward Forty-Eighth Street and they started their walk. "Do you always go out for lunch?"

"No, not usually. I was in a stuffy meeting all morning. It feels good to get some fresh air."

Tony choked out a laugh. "In this city?"

She laughed with him, the early afternoon sun glinting on her hair, picking up different shades of gold. Her teeth were perfectly white and her creamy skin was flawless. Somehow she seemed to keep getting prettier every time he saw her.

"Look, I should warn you, there might be a wait," he said "but we can always catch a taxi for the return trip."

"We? I got the impression last night that you liked to cut and run."

Thank God he didn't blush. "About that," he said. "The real reason I asked you to lunch."

"I thought it might be."

"You don't sound angry…"

"I'm not. Curious. Puzzled. Not angry, though. Which is lucky for you," she said, weaving her way around a sudden influx of pedestrians that pushed between them. When she got close again—almost touching—she went on with her sentence as if it had never stopped. "Because I know two of your secrets. Imagine what I could do if my feathers were ruffled."

"I walked right into that, didn't I?"

"Yes, you did."

He touched the small of her back, his hand acting on its own before he'd remembered his mental vow not to do that again. Catherine didn't seem to mind, though, so he figured a sudden retreat would only make things worse. They turned the corner to an equally busy street. "It's just down there. The one with the sandwich board outside."

"It's a storefront?"

He nodded. "There are a few tables inside, but I wouldn't hold out too much hope of getting one. See all those folks standing near the street? Eating?" Everyone was leaning forward as they ate so they wouldn't get any grease on their business clothes.

"I do. I'm starting to believe you're not the only person who thinks this pizza is the greatest." She curled a hand around his arm. "Let's hurry and get in line."

Tony felt the soft warmth of her palm pressed against his skin.

He grinned all the way to Sunday.

IT WAS BY far the best slice of pizza she'd ever had. She wasn't sure why. Totally worth eating standing outside, trying not to interfere with the pedestrian traffic. The pizza didn't appear to be anything special. But that first bite. She'd made a sound that was absolutely obscene, but was fortunately masked by several other people doing the same.

Even Tony, who'd clearly eaten there many times before and was into his third or fourth bite, groaned in a way she hoped would be repeated while doing things other than eating a slice of cheese pizza.

She leaned close and whispered, "Someone should set up a microphone out here. The porn industry would probably pay a lot for the free background noise."

Tony coughed. He took a quick sip of his soda, upon which he'd been balancing his plate, then coughed again.

Catherine placed a hand on his back, prepared to offer assistance if the need arose.

His face turned an interesting shade of red as he tried to swallow. But at least the coughing had subsided. And so had the stares.

"Yeah, I shouldn't have said that." After giving him a smile, she lowered her lashes and her hand. "Sorry."

He cleared his throat and started laughing.

She took a small bite and chewed like a perfect lady.

"Want another slice?" Tony asked. "Before the line gets longer."

She wanted more than that. A large pie to go would be great, even though she'd have to empty out her small fridge. "Not for me, thanks. But I don't mind waiting if you want another."

"Are you kidding? I don't think I can ever eat pizza in front of you again."

"Oh, come on. It was sort of funny," she said, and took her last bite.

"It was very funny. Just unexpected."

Catherine smiled again. "Finish eating and I promise not to say another word."

Tony lifted one dark brow at her and the way he did it was kind of sexy. She wasn't sure what it meant, but who cared?

The thought stopped her. For someone who made her living reading people, that last thought was like blasphemy. But the truth remained, she continued to miss all but the most blatant signals. Last night, for instance... the way he'd left her on the rooftop had really floored her. And now this...

She truly hoped this lunch wasn't merely an attempt to save face for his family's business.

"So, was this a social call or did you have something to report on the restoration?" she asked, tossing her napkin and paper plate into the trash.

He thought about it as he finished chewing. "Both, I guess," he said, and got rid of his trash as they started walking back. "I called George this morning, and you'll have to wait another week for him to finish the job he's on. As for the garden, I'd recommend Luca taking over the project. He's brilliant at design and he's on his way to finishing his architecture degree, so you'd luck out with him."

She slowed to a stop, causing the man behind her to cuss her out in Castilian Spanish. "So you're—"

Tony held up a hand, and the tight ball in her chest eased into something that allowed her to breathe.

"I've never done anything like that before. Kissing a client is completely unprofessional. And pretty crazy."

They started walking again. Well, he did, and she scurried to catch up.

"And to leave the way I did? I feel like every kind of fool." He stopped. Forcing her to piss off more New Yorkers. No one seemed to be mad at him, though.

"The worst thing is I'd do it again. I want to do it again right now. I'm very attracted to you, and I was reasonably sure I was getting the right signals back, but what I did was not cool. So, whatever happens, I wanted to make sure you knew I was sorry."

Catherine wasn't sure she heard everything past the part where he'd said he wanted to kiss her right now.

Tony studied her. "I thought we were doing okay today, but maybe I misread things again," he said, when she didn't respond. "Look, I can get you a cab, send you back to work. Then you could let me know, whenever it's comfortable, what you want to do."

"Or I could tell you right now."

He blinked. "Now would be great. But…there's more. Even if Luca took over and we started hooking up—whatever that entails—you'd still be a client and that makes things tricky." They stopped at the intersection and he lowered his voice even more. "Little Italy is a small community, and it gets even smaller when you try to keep people out of your business."

"Is that it?"

"Pretty much. Yeah." His eyebrows drew together in a suspicious frown when she stepped closer to him instead of following the crowd when the light changed.

There were far too many people around for this conversation, so she pulled Tony up against the window of a copy store, away from foot traffic. "What if I just fired you?"

He let out a sigh. "Shit. Seriously?"

"It would solve just about everything, right?"

He deflated. Briefly laid his head back against the brick and studied her. Her teasing gaze must have given her away. He straightened and narrowed his eyes. "Hey, this isn't easy. I've never kissed a client before."

"Sorry. That was a joke," she said. "I'm actually wondering why we can't do both."

"Both…?"

"Why can't we continue to work together?"

"And the other thing would be…"

"I think you know."

Tony grinned, looking just too damned adorable for words.

"There's no rule, is there? I mean, you won't be expelled from the contractors' guild or anything?"

"No. There's no rule. But give me a minute, okay?" he said. "My heart nearly exploded when you said you'd fire us. I was already trying to figure out how to explain that one to my family."

Catherine smiled big. Nice to know he would've chosen her over the job. "I wasn't trying to get even, but I do want you to stay involved in the restoration. Nothing against Luca…"

"Fair enough," Tony said, getting some of his composure back. "More than fair. If we see that our personal relationship is affecting the work, we'll take a step back. Reevaluate the situation."

"One would hope we could be that mature about it."

"Right," he said with a wry laugh. "For now I'm giving you a heads-up, in case you see anyone from your office around."

"A heads-up for…?" she asked slowly, the intent in his eyes sending a shiver of anticipation down her spine.

Tony smiled. "I think you know."

He pulled her into his arms. Nothing that would cause the crowd to pause, but it felt wonderful. "I'd like to start right now," he said, his whisper close to her ear, "but I'll settle for tomorrow night. How would you feel about skipping our work session tonight and coming over to my place for dinner tomorrow night instead?"

She looked up into his beautiful dark eyes, appreciating again his laugh lines, and his unaffected grin. "I'm sure that can be arranged."

He showed his approval with a kiss that wasn't nearly as desperate as the one on the rooftop. It started off with a brush of his lips, a taste of his breath, the warmth of his body. She followed him easily. In fact, it was the deepest connection she'd felt to him so far. There wasn't one awkward thing about it. Not the quick swipe of his tongue across her lower lip, not the moan only she could hear.

She sighed into him, and he held her tighter. Finally, he did the gentlemanly thing and pulled back. "Now there's no question I'll need to hail a cab for you so you won't be late. Mind if I hitch a ride?"

"Not at all. But don't you have an appointment coming up?"

"Yeah," he said, pulling her through a brief break in the pedestrian traffic until he could thrust his arm out for a taxi. "But later. At the office. That's why I can't help out at your place tonight."

"Huh. I was going to ask you to come into the UN for the ten-cent tour, but now that I know you lied, I'm not going to."

"You know, I really would like to see the inside," he said. "I don't really know what you do, except that it has something to do with translation."

"Something like that, yes. I'll explain tomorrow evening, if that's all right?" Despite her desire to show him her workplace they'd actually used up too much of her lunch break eating and talking. Which was fine, since she had a lot of work to do. Although trying to concentrate after what just happened? That would be a real feat.

6

THE NEXT MORNING Catherine stopped at the closest news-stand, bought two magazines and a London *Times*. After she'd paid the nice man who ran the kiosk, she was surprised to bump into a woman she recognized. It was her neighbor on the other side. She had a red front door and a large pot of marigolds on the stoop. At least Catherine thought it was her neighbor. So many of the older women had the same outdated hairstyle, hair severely pulled back into a tight bun.

Still, Catherine smiled at her. "Good morning."

The woman looked at her as if she was insulted by the greeting. She did give Catherine a brief nod, however, before she summoned an actual smile for the kiosk man. Either Catherine had been mistaken and the woman wasn't her neighbor, or else she'd managed to alienate the entire neighborhood with all the noise. But even so, the woman could have been a little more pleasant.

Later, Catherine spent her lunch hour standing in line at yet another bakery—this time, the Lady M Boutique in Bryant Park. She knew a little bit more about what Tony liked, so she'd narrowed her choices for their dessert down to four kinds of cake.

She hoped the line would move quickly, as she wanted to get back to work as soon as possible. Which didn't mean she would be able to do any work. She'd been so distracted ever since yesterday, it was a little crazy.

After Sal and his crew had left, she'd worked on the upstairs fireplace tile—a horrid, messy job that required more muscle than care. Not really her cup of tea, but once she'd started, she pressed on. Plenty of time to let her thoughts wander, and of course, they'd zeroed in on Tony.

It helped that she'd listened to Marvin Gaye. God, such sexy music. And then she'd taken a long, slow bath in oil-rich water, using her fingers as a pale substitute as she tried to imagine what sex would be like with Tony.

But it wasn't until she'd slipped between her sheets that she realized the depth of the opportunity that had been handed to her. Tony wasn't just gorgeous. He was bright and funny and he lived what she considered to be a real life. At least compared to what she was used to. Of course, she'd known people from all social classes, but her past relationships and all her friends and associates had some kind of tie to her rarified world.

The kind of money her family had was used to a great extent to set them apart, to cushion them from the harsh realities of 99 percent of the population. At least her family had always stressed service as a fundamental precept. But for the most part, their charity was performed at arm's length. Usually, they just made big monetary donations.

Even the men she'd seen socially she'd met at school or through cocktail parties and charity dinners. She'd had some interesting dates, two longer-term relationships with men she liked, but nothing that had rocked her world.

Tony had to be more experienced than she was, and

she really looked forward to getting to know him, and not just sexually, either. She tried to think of another man she'd ever been this intrigued by, and couldn't.

It was her turn to order, so she stepped up to the counter. "I'd like four different slices to go, please." She grinned as she made her selections, and blushed all the way back to the UN, thinking about what it would be like when she and Tony got between the sheets.

TONY HAD LEFT work on the early side. Poor Gina must have suspected he was going to see a woman tonight, and her level of curiosity hinted that she knew it wasn't going to be Rita.

He was used to the fact that practically everyone knew about his arrangement with Rita despite the fact he'd never told anyone, and he knew Rita hadn't, either. They'd barely been out together. Usually she'd come to his apartment and they'd have food delivered. But that didn't stop the gossip mill.

Sometimes he hated the tiny community he lived in. He barely had any time to enjoy being in the most exciting city in the world, so it wasn't as if it was a trade-off. He just wished that people would mind their own damn business.

As soon as he got home, he relaxed. At least to a degree. Knowing he'd be with Catherine soon was damned exciting, but it was the good kind of tension. He looked forward to showing her his home. It was the place he loved the most, and he knew she'd understand what it meant to him. It was far enough away from work that the claustrophobic attention he was normally paid was greatly reduced. And after the divorce, he'd decorated to his tastes, not Angie's.

He checked on the bottle of Syrah he'd uncorked a

half hour ago, then checked the time and hurried to take a shower. As it got closer to Catherine's arrival, he became more anxious. Anticipation had him humming as he got dressed, and to his surprise it wasn't just about the hoped-for sex at the end of the evening. There was so much he didn't know about Catherine.

As they'd planned, she called him when she arrived on his block. He took the elevator down to the lobby of his building and met her at the door. Catherine surprised him with a very European greeting, an almost-kiss on each cheek. She also had a pastry box in her hand from a shop he didn't recognize.

"What a gorgeous neighborhood," she said, as he led her to the elevator. "There's only one button. Is this a private elevator?"

"Yes, it is."

"Are you in the penthouse?"

"Nope. The eighth floor. It's an unusual building. The eighth, in my opinion, is the best of the lot."

He could see her reevaluating him, wide-eyed, as they went up floor by floor. Completely understandable. "The area is called the Cast Iron Historic District. I figured you'd like it. This building is prewar, but there's been a lot of work done."

"I was impressed on the cab ride here. Stunning architecture. No wonder you know so much about restoration. You never said you had your own historic treasure."

He held the door open for her as they entered the living room. It was a completely open plan all the way to the kitchen. The showstoppers were the twelve-foot vaulted ceilings and the double-arched wood casement windows. Above his oversize custom sofa he had a large print of an architectural jewel from Barcelona, one of Antoni Gaudí's mosaic arches. The walls were white, the floor-to-ceiling drapes were white and gray, and both offset the dark wood floors.

She walked over to the farthest window and stared at the view for several moments. Without disturbing her too much, he took her jacket, purse and the bakery box and put them on his big dining table. He stood by her again, quietly letting her look around while he watched her.

She looked beautiful in a demure black dress that hit her midknee. It had some lace up at the top, which was nice, too, but what he liked the most were her fire-engine-red heels.

Damn, he wanted her to like what she saw. He was proud of the place. The work he'd put into it had been significant, and thankfully, Angie had been fine about him keeping it. Maybe if they'd had kids, it would have been different, but this had been his pet project before they'd decided to get married.

"I'm sorry, this is the rudest question I've ever asked. But, your business is this good?"

"It's very good, but this building is owned by my family. Has been for generations. I did a lot of the renovations myself."

"It's fantastic."

"Thank you. Now, if you don't have any objections, I'd like to kiss you. The anticipation is getting out of hand."

She turned right into his arms, her smile almost as welcoming as her sparkling eyes.

He meant to approach her with a slow burn that would last through dinner, but the moment she parted her lips for him, he abandoned his plan. Her response was better than he'd hoped for. Their tongues touched and tangled. She met him stroke for stroke as he explored her mouth, sampling her sweetness. As he ran his hands over her, he felt a tremor run all the way down her spine. She pulled him tighter against her body, and now he could feel the vibration through his clothes and hers.

Jesus. She'd just gotten here. The urge to pick her up and take her straight to his bed was strong, but he dialed it down about twenty degrees because that wasn't all he wanted from her. He hadn't been a teenager for a long time, although it felt as if he'd suddenly reverted to seventeen.

It was everything he could do to gently disengage from the bonfire he'd started. He didn't want this to be a wham-bam-thank-you-ma'am event. She was worth more than that to him.

"Wine?" he said.

She licked her lips, which didn't help him cool down at all. "Yes, please."

"I hope you like Syrah."

"I do. Very much."

She walked next to him into the kitchen. "It smells wonderful in here."

"You hungry?"

Her nod wasn't all that convincing. But maybe that had to do with the fact that she couldn't stop staring at him. Of course, he stared right back. He was normally a patient man, but if he didn't do something soon...

Wine.

He still needed to pour her some. Maybe drink some himself. Talk to the woman. Put her at ease.

She brought her glass up for a toast. "To new adventures."

He couldn't argue with that. They clicked and sipped.

"Very nice wine."

"I'm glad you like it. So, about what you do?"

"Ah. I'm primarily a terminologist. Although I worked for several years as a translator. And I've also studied kinesics, interpretations of body language, so sometimes I'm called in to help with that. "

"I've heard of everything but being a terminologist."

"It's not a common career. I read a lot of newspapers from around the world, watch current television programming and films from different countries, read novels by international authors and try to keep abreast of all the changes in words, tone and nuance. My colleagues and I do our best to standardize the six languages approved by the UN, but any new information about words and their meanings can help everyone and the process in general."

"That makes sense. It would be important to understand the nuances when you're dealing with politicians "

"Exactly. Nuance can mean the difference between war and peace."

"With those skills, I'd ask what you've learned about me, but I don't think I want to know."

Oddly, a pink blush tinted her cheeks before she said, "I wouldn't be here if I didn't think good things."

"Huh. I'm glad." He wanted to shift the conversation. Although he found her fascinating, he wasn't sure how his background could possibly stand up to the life she'd lived. "So, how many languages do you speak?"

"Four, including three of the official six languages of the UN."

"Which are?"

"English, Russian and French."

"And the fourth?"

"Italian," she said.

"Whoa. I can barely manage two. English and cussing."

She laughed. "Having an ear isn't a requirement of the job, but it helps immensely."

"What was your first language? I mean, what did you speak while you were growing up?"

"English and French, pretty much equally."

"You don't have an accent." He drank some more wine, offered to top her up, but she waved the bottle away. "Well, not exactly," he said, "but you sound like you might be from Europe."

"That's not an actual accent."

"I don't know. There's a little BBC, a little American newscaster and maybe some French in there."

Her brow furrowed.

"That first day I met you, when you said *'accoutrements'*..."

"Oh, right. I have a thing for beautiful words in whatever language I find prettiest." Catherine smiled. "That was excellent pronunciation, by the way."

"I don't know why. I can't seem to get a handle on Italian. I understand most of it. Just can't form sentences. And here you can speak it. Go ahead, put me to shame."

Catherine laughed again. Her eyes sparkled and her skin seemed to glow, and he had no idea how much longer he could keep his hands off her.

He took another sip of wine. "You sound as if you really enjoy your work."

"I do. The UN is exciting and for the most part I like the people I work with. They even offer free classes to all their employees, so I take advantage of their programs."

"I'm embarrassed to admit I've never been there. You'd think I would have, growing up so close."

"I'll take you. It'll be better than the general tour. I know a lot about the design and architecture of the building."

"Oh, baby, you know what I like."

The way she looked at him now had nothing at all to do with her job. "I've been thinking a lot about tonight," she said, and moistened her lips. "Ever since you asked me over."

After putting his glass down, he plucked hers from her hand and set it next to his.

SHE COULD HARDLY BREATHE, there was so much electricity swirling between them.

The way he caressed her cheek and the sizzling look in his eyes asked her for permission to continue without saying a single word. As she nodded, his other hand went around her waist to pull her close.

He leaned in until she could smell the wine on his breath, but then he surprised her by moving his head lower. Starting with the hollow of her neck, he laid soft, tiny kisses all the way up her neck to her chin.

Her eyes nearly rolled back in their sockets, but she got her bearings quickly when he changed his target. After sweeping his tongue over her bottom lip, he slipped it inside her mouth. She made a sound, something from deep in her chest, which made him hold her tighter. His erection pressed against the top of her thigh and as he made love to her mouth, he shifted until he could rock against the top of her pussy.

"Come to my bed," he whispered, just before he nipped her right earlobe. "I want to strip you down to your heels. Make you come every way there is."

The invitation lit up more erogenous zones than she'd known she had. She nodded, hitting his nose with her own. It hurt.

"Ow," he said, but it didn't stop him from grabbing hold of her buttocks and lifting her up onto the kitchen counter.

She gasped at the move, at his heat, at the hands running up her thighs, sneaking underneath her dress. It al-

lowed her to spread her legs only a bit, but Tony didn't
seem to mind. When he reached the limit of his fingertips, he started pushing up her dress a little at a time.

Her soft gasp made him freeze, but she kissed him
again as quickly as she could. She'd thought about un-
dressing for him, but this could be better. It all depended
on what he was going to do when the dress reached the
top of her thighs.

It was interesting to kiss his smile. Had she honestly
never kissed a man who was grinning? Because she
could, she traced the edges of his upturned lips with
her tongue.

That made him moan, which made her want to squeeze
her legs together. Of course she couldn't, which turned
out to be surprisingly hot. He kept inching her dress up,
but unless she balanced on her hands he wasn't going to
succeed. "Tony?"

"Hmm?" He nibbled at a very tender spot below her
ear.

"The dress is too long for this to work."

His lips stopped moving. "I really liked this idea. It
was supposed to make you swoon."

"You succeeded too well, I think…" She slipped her
hands between them and began unbuttoning his silky
shirt. It wasn't easy, but she was determined. When she'd
done as much as she could, her hand slid down over his
pants so she could feel his length. And girth. Impressive.
As was the growl in his moan.

For a moment, he barely moved, except for his quick-
ening breath. She could probably make him come like
this, just rubbing him off, but that was for another time.

She slid her hand up again, and he huffed a deep breath
as she pulled his shirt free of his pants. That spurred him
into a whole new gear.

After helping her down from the counter, he took her hand and walked her through the dining room, down a hallway with several doors, all the way back to the master suite.

"I'm so glad you're here," he said, his mouth meeting hers, opening, parting, then finding her again at a different angle.

"Me, too," she whispered.

Tony took hold of the hem of her dress, abandoning his slow pace. He bunched the material in his hand and pulled the dress up to midthigh, while kissing her hard and deep.

Her breath caught, and she wasn't at all sure how long she could remain standing. Wet and aching, desperately wanting them both naked, she got busy with his shirt once more.

Warm fingers moved up her stocking, pausing as he reached the lace at the top. "What's this?" he said, his voice lower and a good deal rougher.

"I'll bet you can figure it out."

He met her gaze with very dark eyes and a slightly furrowed brow. He stared, unblinking, as he explored what he couldn't see.

The second he realized there was almost nothing above the thigh-high stockings, his eyes widened. "Are you…"

She grinned at him, finally getting his belt out of the way. Before she could get hold of his top pants button, he dropped. Straight down so that he was eye level with her crotch, although he was looking up at her face.

Carefully, he reached his right hand underneath her dress and ran one finger across the top of her stocking. His gaze didn't waver, not even a flicker, and she couldn't help but spread her legs a little more, her heart beating strong and fast in her chest. Still, he didn't look. He felt.

The clever man moved his hand to her side and ran it up until he reached the satin string on her hip. "I'm going to say…red."

She lifted her eyebrows, not willing to give anything away. But instead of verifying his guess, he surprised her again. He followed the crease between thigh and torso until two fingers slipped underneath the tiny patch of silk that was the biggest part of her thong. She inhaled sharply as he skimmed her trimmed lower lips, then dipped inside.

"God," she whispered, finding this game unbearably sexy.

"Oh, Christ, you're so ready for me."

"Sometimes teasing is nice," she said, putting her hand on the back of his head.

"And sometimes, one of us can't crouch down like this without hurting ourselves." He winced, and used his left hand to adjust his fly. He also slid his fingers out of her, then rose, taking her dress with him. She lifted her arms and a moment later she was in her heels, lace-trimmed stockings, itty-bitty red thong and a ridiculously expensive matching red demi bra.

Tony's groan sounded as if it had risen all the way from his toes. "You are stunning," he said, "and I can't take it for one more second."

Before she could make sense of what he'd said, he yanked the comforter back so hard it nearly flew off the mattress. Then she was in his arms, being settled on his king-size bed so her head rested on his pillow.

He stripped in what had to be record time, and okay, she hadn't underestimated his enthusiasm. His cock was hard, standing so tall it brushed the skin below his belly button. He rubbed it once, baring his teeth, then held his arms down, his hands fisted by his sides. "What do you want?"

"You, in the bed with me," she said, scooting over a few inches.

"Is that all?"

She gave him a wicked smile. "For starters."

7

Tony opened his bedside drawer and pulled out a bunch of condoms, which he dumped on top of the table, then snatched one back just as he climbed onto the bed. He was at the edge of being too turned on. The same woman who'd worn the black skirt and white blouse was about to be all his, looking as sexy as anything he'd ever seen.

He'd meant to have dinner first. Talk more. Get to know each other better. What an idiot. Of course he hadn't been able to keep his hands off her. Or his mouth. Although he supposed this was just another way of becoming acquainted.

Moving closer, he looked at her again in her tiny bra and thong, and his cock jerked, insistent that he get on with it. He couldn't argue the point. Although damn it, he wasn't going to last.

"I meant," he said, as he touched her chest with his fingertips, tracing the skin above her bra, "what do you *want*?"

She reached for his hand, then guided his fingers underneath the bra. Her nipple was hard, and he wanted to taste it. He used his knuckles to push down the red satin until he could see his targets. Mesmerized, he found his mouth watering as he got closer, until he was able to touch that peaked flesh with the tip of his tongue.

Her gasp wasn't loud, but it hit him hard. He sucked the nub between his lips, swirled his tongue, ached for the bra to be off, for all of her to be spread out for him.

The way her back arched when he flicked her nipple made him ache, but he had to stop, do something about his cock before he had an accident.

He reared up, tore open the condom, hissed as he rolled it down onto his cock. "Please don't think this is my usual tempo," he said, as he moved himself between her thighs. "I swear I can take my time. Just not now."

"Thank God," she said, arching again, reaching behind her back to unhook her bra. "I'm about ready to burst, myself."

He grinned, bumped into the patch of thong covering her pussy and quickly shoved that to the side. "Damn it, Catherine," he said, holding himself carefully as he rubbed between her lips. "So hot, so wet. I can't—"

The moment he dipped inside her, it was almost all over. Somehow, he managed to enter her completely, feeling the tight sweet heat grip him until white spots hit him behind his eyelids. He hadn't remembered closing his eyes, and he rectified that instantly, needing to see.

She stole his breath, literally. He couldn't breathe for a long, long moment, and then she gasped as he began to move. Every part of him wanted to push with all his might, but he controlled himself. At first.

Then she lifted her hips to meet him on the next thrust, and all his noble ideas went to hell.

Her mouth opened as he thrust into her, balancing on his knees and one hand, teasing her nipple with the other. He wanted to kiss her, but couldn't seem to make that work, so he just stared at the flush that painted her cheeks pink, the sounds—moans mixed with higher-pitched cries—all of them turning him inside out.

He just couldn't hold back another minute.

Needing to hold on to the bed, he let go of her breast. Once he was grounded, she met him thrust for thrust, groan for groan. Her hair spilled all over his pillow, her legs wrapped around his hips and nothing existed except their bodies and his desperate need to stay inside her all night long.

He lasted longer than he'd thought possible. Until she made an unearthly sound and nearly bucked him off. His orgasm nearly made him black out, it was so strong. He could barely hear, the blood rushing too loudly in his ears, couldn't see, with the flashes that hit behind his eyes.

Then…stillness.

He was in her as far as he could possibly go. Her back arched and her nails gripped his shoulders hard enough to bruise. Although her lips had parted, no sounds escaped except for her rapid, desperate breaths.

Finally, he inhaled, so deeply it felt like fire in his lungs, and pulled out before he fell like a log on top of her.

Luckily, he didn't land on anything important. The two of them sounded as if they'd just run a marathon, but the high was infinitely better. He threaded his fingers through hers. "You okay?"

She turned her head so they were looking right at each other. "More than."

"Good."

"But a little shivery."

"Right. I'm going to get up. Really, really soon and get the comforter over you."

"Take your time. I'm fine. Oh, God, I'm still wearing my heels."

"They're very nice heels. They go with your delicates."

"My delicates?"

He shrugged. "'Underwear' didn't have quite the zing I was looking for."

Her stomach gurgled, and her eyes got wide. "Sorry about that."

"No, you must be starving. Look, the bathroom is through that door." He pointed as he got out of bed and wrestled with the comforter. "You get yourself comfortable, and I'm going to bring food. And drink."

"Okay."

He snatched his robe off the back of his bedroom door, and then stopped by the other bathroom before he made his way to the kitchen, the pastry box too tempting to ignore.

Inside, four amazing-looking slices of cake were packed with great care. The hell with his earlier plans. He grabbed the bottle of wine, their glasses, two forks, and headed back, careful with the box.

She was under the covers, leaning on a pillow against the headboard. The minute she saw what he'd brought she burst out laughing. "Dessert first?"

"Why not? We're grown-ups. We can do what we want."

"As long as you brought two forks, I'm in."

"I couldn't stand it," he said. "I had to look, and then there was no going back. I mean, we can eat dinner later, right?"

"Absolutely."

He put the box next to her on the bed, then handed her the almost empty glass she'd used before. "It must have been fate that I chose this Syrah. It goes really well with dessert."

"I believe you," she said, holding her glass higher.

He poured, then filled his own glass, handed her the forks and, realizing what he'd forgotten, went into the en suite and got a fresh box of tissues. "I know the kitchen isn't that far, and I could have brought napkins—"

"But this seems much more daring."

"Exactly."

Once his robe dropped, he climbed into the bed next to her. The first thing he did was point to the green cake. "Green?"

"Green tea mille crêpes. Not too sweet. But rich."

Pretty sure he knew what to expect, he cut off a bite. It was really good. Unusual. Classy. Just like Catherine. Once he swallowed, he waited for her to take her bite. She took a sizable chunk, yet still managed to look elegant. "I know some things about your taste," he said, "and now I have a pretty good idea about your work, but there's a lot of territory between birth and working at the UN that we still haven't covered."

She stopped chewing and stared. "You want me to tell you everything that's happened to me since birth?"

He laughed. "No. Just the highlights. In fact, just whatever you want to tell me. But before we do…" He leaned over and kissed her, finding the taste of sweet cream on her lips. "I don't think I told you how often I've thought about tonight."

"Me, too. Made a mistake at work today, wondering where you called home. I was way off the mark."

"Good different or bad different?"

She laughed, the sound hitting him low down in his chest. "Good. Very good."

"Now, tell me more about yourself."

"Okay," she said, but she took a bite from the chocolate cake before she started. The way she studied him made him wonder if she'd begin at the beginning or keep her past to herself.

"I was born in Lichtenstein," she said. "Although I'm an American citizen. My father was the ambassador when my parents had me. We traveled a great deal, all over Europe."

"Siblings?"

"None. I had tutors, though. Nannies. Housekeepers. Didn't spend a lot of time with my parents. They both went to a lot of meetings, attended a lot of parties. My mother was born in France, my father in California. They met while studying at the Harvard University Kennedy School of Government. Mother became an American citizen, and before having me, she worked for the French embassy in DC, while my father was a personal assistant to the secretary of state."

"So a lot like my family."

She grinned. "I think you probably had a much happier childhood than I did. Not complaining, exactly, but it was a very formal way to live." Her gaze moved away from him. Not far. Just to the cake, although she didn't take another bite. "I always felt as though my family was born in the wrong century. I had to learn early how to use every possible utensil, I started studying up on wines when I was ten, and my parents were very pleased that I picked up languages so easily. They wanted me to follow in their footsteps."

"They must be thrilled about your work at the UN."

Her wince told another story. "They think I'm wasting my talents."

"Well, parents. They're…"

"A long way away, which is how I like it."

Tony loved his folks, but he could understand that. "Which was your favorite country?"

"Right now? America. But I loved Italy. Switzerland was cold. France…well, who doesn't love France. And the British Isles were pretty fantastic."

"I envy your travels."

"Don't you ever go on vacation?"

"Yeah. But not overseas. Someday I'll go." He waited, smiling, as she took a pretty big bite of the strawberry cake. "Has anyone ever called you anything but Catherine?"

"Like…?"

"Cat? Cathy? Cate? My liege?"

"That last one. All the time. It's a burden I'm forced to bear."

"I'll bet."

After another bite, she put down her fork. "I've only been called Catherine. Except for one person. Belaflore Calabrese."

"Who told you stories about Little Italy?"

"That's right. She was very, very dear to me. The best part of my life, really. I was always well behaved when she was our housekeeper, afraid she'd be fired like so many others. But luckily, she became my nanny and stayed with us through all our travels. She used to come here for her vacations, to see her family who lived in the house that's now mine. It's awful to admit, but I was always jealous. I wanted to be her only family."

"You were just a kid."

"I know." Catherine sighed. "That's not why I bought the house. There's nothing Freudian to worry about."

Tony smiled. "What did she call you?"

"La mia patatina," she said, her voice at least half an octave higher. "It means—"

"My little potato? Is that right?" He frowned when she

nodded. "That's not one I've heard a lot around here. But I'm guessing it's nice."

"Very nice. But she also called me *tesorina* and *topolina*. Always a whisper just between the two of us. If I have any sentimentality, it's because of Mia Nonnina. She nurtured my heart for many years."

He swallowed his latest bite, sipped his wine and then asked, "So you knew the Calabrese family before you bought the house?"

"That's right. They knew I wanted it, and offered it to me before they put it on the market. I paid what they asked. It was a no-brainer for me. I'd already gotten the job in New York, though I hadn't started there yet. They also warned me about the condition of the place, but as you well know, I don't mind. Even if I never did another thing with that house, I'd love it. Every time I'm there, I walk with the memory of Belaflore. Told you. Sentimental."

"I understand." His words were soft as he leaned in. "I come from the most sentimental people in the world. Can't even talk without using my hands." To demonstrate, he cupped her cheek and brought her in for a long, sweet kiss. When he let her go, he put his fork down, too. "You know, I've got one of my mom's lasagnas warming in the oven. Any interest?"

"A lot of interest. I like this whole eating dessert first, though. I'll have to do it more often."

He got out of bed and opened the closet door. It was a ridiculously large walk-in, pure cedar, with enough room for a family of four. But he had a second robe in there that shouldn't be too big for Catherine.

By the time he got back to the bed, she'd put the cake box next to the wine bottle and was holding her bra and dress.

"Maybe this instead of getting dressed? I'd hate to get any sauce on your beautiful clothes."

She tossed them both on the bed. "Thanks. Great idea. And maybe you'll show me the rest of the house on our way to the kitchen?"

"One tour, coming up."

As they put on their respective robes, he said, "You'll appreciate the closet."

Catherine walked around the bed and gasped as soon as she looked inside. "It's as big as most New York apartments."

"When I have time, I'm going to make most of it into an office."

"And here I am, keeping you busy helping me with my house when you want to work on your own."

"It's not a problem," he said, waving it away. "You've seen the bathroom?"

"Yes. It's quite impressive. And the marble is stunning."

"My ex's—Angie's—favorite. I got to choose the shower, though."

Catherine stared at him. "Your ex-wife?"

Tony had to give her credit; she'd never asked after meeting Mrs. Collette. "I'm divorced. Is that a problem?"

"No. I mean…" Catherine shook her head. "Not for me, it isn't. I expected so." She smiled. "It's fine."

He started to let it go, but knew damn well the remark would bother him. "Expected it?"

"Come on…a great guy like you? Good-looking. Smart. Successful. Someone was bound to—"

"Okay." He laughed at his own embarrassment. "Before you ask, the split was amicable. No kids involved. It's all good. You want to see more of the place?"

"Of course I do." Smiling, Catherine stretched up and

brushed her lips across his mouth. But when the kiss got heated she backed off. "Show me."

Deciding to let her get away with the dodge for now, he led her down the long hall, stopping at the guest bedroom with its en suite, and another smaller bedroom. Then they walked back into the large open space that was a living room, dining room and kitchen all in one.

"This space is out of this world. I love the art, by the way. Gaudí is a favorite of mine."

"There was an exhibit of his stuff at the Met. I liked it a lot."

They walked past the big dining table, one he'd built when he was twenty, then into the kitchen, with its wide island and stainless appliances.

"This is a total chef's kitchen," she said. "I recognize the brands of the stove and the fridge. Do you cook often?"

"Not really. I can make a decent omelet, a steak and pasta. Everything else I bring in. Including tonight's dinner. I didn't even make the salad."

"No harm in that. I think I want to steal your entire kitchen for my place, though. It's stunning."

"This was all my ex-wife's doing. She's the one who chose everything even though she was a terrible cook. I've been able to figure out how to get around in here for two years, though, with no problems. So if you want this configuration, we can certainly accommodate that."

He got the lasagna out of the oven, pulled down a couple plates and cut them each a big piece.

"I'll never be able to eat all that."

"I don't know. You're living in Little Italy now. It's not a meal until you've eaten twice your weight in pasta."

"Damn. I guess I'll have to join a gym."

"It's inevitable," he said, getting them both forks. They

didn't even move to the table. Just leaned over the island and dug in.

She took a bite and her eyes widened almost comically, then she took two more bites in quick succession. "Tony," she said, as if she was about to impart some huge news. "This is the best lasagna I've ever had. Your mother is an amazing cook."

"She learned from my grandmother, who lives with them. When my brothers and I were growing up, every day was like a cook-off. It was actually pretty insane."

"That must be tough on—"

She stopped talking when the elevator dinged.

Tony groaned. "Oh, shit. I'm sorry about this," he said, walking across the room. He knew who it was. The only other person to have a key. His brother Dom. Because he was still in school, he lived with their folks, but he liked to crash in the guest room from time to time. He usually called before he came, though.

"Yo, Tony," he said, walking in like he owned the place, his gym bag in hand. "It smells like Ma's lasagna. Thank God, I'm starving."

"Why didn't you call?"

"I left two messages."

"And my not returning them didn't give you a clue?"

Dominic looked him over, finally noticing that Tony was in his bathrobe, barefoot. Then he obviously caught sight of Catherine. "Oh. Shit. Sorry, bro. Seriously. Hey, how you doing?" he said, over Tony's shoulder. "Sorry to barge in."

"It's fine," Catherine said, but Tony could hear that it wasn't.

"So?"

Dom winced. "You think maybe you could cut me a couple slices before I leave? Ma's pissed at me, so I'm gonna have to stay at Mikey's, and he never has anything to eat."

"Go. Away."

"You know what?" Catherine said. "I was just about to leave myself. You don't have to go. It's getting late. I'll just be a few more minutes."

Tony turned to see her hurrying toward his bedroom. "Goddamn it, Dom. Get your food and get the hell out."

Dom's free hand went up in surrender. "Hey. I'm really sorry. I had no idea you wouldn't be alone." He leaned in closer. "And with the Fox, no less. Whoa."

Tony held himself back from punching his little brother into next week. "It isn't what you think and you will never bring it up again. Are we clear?"

"Like she spilled something on all her clothes? After she came over to talk about restoring fireplaces?"

"Dom. I swear to God…"

Dom got down one of the big dinner plates, took almost half the damn lasagna in one messy scoop and then covered it with aluminum foil. He spotted the open bottle of wine and raised his eyebrows at his brother.

All Tony could do was point to the door. "Last chance, or I push you out the window."

"Fine, fine. Don't get all bent. I'm leaving." Dom hurried to the elevator, but as the doors were closing, he said, "Sure I shouldn't go say good-night to your—"

Thankfully, the door shut on his big mouth.

Now, damage control. Tony hurried down the hall, not surprised to see Catherine's clothes and shoes missing, and the bathroom door shut. He tapped on it. "You okay?"

"Of course," she said, as she opened the door. She looked elegant as always. Too bad he couldn't help imagining her without the dress. He'd wanted to do so much more.

"Sure you can't stay? You barely had any dinner."

"No, I'm going to go. I'm sorry. It's probably worse for you that we were caught."

"Dom won't say anything. I swear. He knows I'd kill him if he even suggested that you were here."

She walked closer, touched the bare skin above his collarbones. "I had a wonderful time. Truly I did. But I think I need to think this thing through. Okay? How about we give it a day or two—"

"I planned on coming by tomorrow night."

"Maybe…call first, okay?"

"I can't tell you how sorry I am. This is the best night I've had in I don't know how long. I'd very much like to try again."

She kissed his cheek. "We'll see."

"I'll pack up some lasagna and cake to go," he said, attempting to keep his voice light.

"Don't worry about it," she said, walking out of his bedroom. "Enjoy the cakes. I don't think you tried all of them yet."

He followed her, and after she put on her jacket and got her purse, he pressed for the elevator. Gently pushing a stray hair off her temple, he leaned closer. "I'll do whatever you like," he said. "I never wanted to make you feel uncomfortable. But for what it's worth, I feel like tonight was just a tiny taste of what could be a great time for both of us."

She smiled. But when the door slid open, she stepped inside without another word.

8

FINALLY, CATHERINE WAS EXCUSED. She'd just finished interpreting a speech for members of the UN Security Council, which wasn't technically her job any longer. The real reason she'd been asked to translate was to pick up any signals from the body language of the speaker. She'd spent over a week steeped in research, watching tapes over and over again, until she had a solid sense of his style, his use of colloquialisms, his nervous tics.

She walked from the Security Council Chamber to her office. She'd have just enough time to log in and check her email before she had to meet Victor for lunch. She knew he was going to ask her out again, and while she didn't want to date him, she also didn't want there to be tension between them.

Pity she wasn't attracted to him. He was her mother's dream for her, but Catherine just didn't feel a spark. Victor was too much about presentation and not enough about the things that really mattered to her: wit, kindness, keeping an open mind and being comfortable with all manner of people. At times he could be witty, but otherwise, he was, frankly, a snob.

Tony had all the qualities she admired, but while he

wasn't a rube, he was dramatically different from the type of man she usually dated. That fact held a lot of allure.

She'd decided to give the two of them another shot. After two days of talking on the phone—teasing each other and laughing lots—she'd caved, anxious to see him again. Tonight there would be some work on the downstairs fireplace that would hopefully transition to some one-on-one time in the bedroom. This time with no brothers dropping by.

She'd just put her purse in her drawer when her boss, Eugene Tinibu, stopped her. "Could you please come with me to the delegates' lounge? Ambassador Adolphi's wife is having some difficulties with her Russian dress designer."

"Seriously? I've just left the—"

"I realize. But I would appreciate you taking a few moments."

"A few? You know Ambassador Adolphi's wife never uses two words when ten will do, and now you're adding a Russian dress designer to the mix?"

"It's you, or I have to dig up two translators, and all I want, dear God, is to meet my wife for her doctor's appointment. Our first ultrasound of the baby."

Catherine checked her watch. "That's low, Eugene," she said, teasing him. "Using your wife like that. But fine. Go see your baby. And bring back a copy of the picture."

He squeezed her shoulder and dashed off. Of course, she could have mentioned that her lunch plans were at the delegates' dining room, which was near the lounge, so it wasn't really that big of a deal. Although Adolphi's wife was a nightmare.

When Catherine reached the lounge she saw the two women right away. Mrs. Adolphi, a beautiful Italian woman with extravagant tastes, was staring daggers at another beautiful woman who was staring right back. Before Catherine could get a word out, Mrs. Adolphi started speaking to her in Italian and the designer joined in in her native Russian. As the daughter of two career diplomats, Catherine had no trouble shutting them both up. Not five minutes later, she'd figured out that the dispute was based on a simple misunderstanding.

After setting a date and location for the first fitting, both women thanked Catherine and invited her to have drinks with them at an exclusive Manhattan private club.

She declined, of course, in spite of their insistence. Even if Catherine hadn't been meeting Tony later, she'd have had no interest in going to a club with those two. At least she didn't have to rush to make her lunch date.

She arrived five minutes early, but Victor was already waiting for her. As usual, he looked the picture of sophistication in his charcoal-gray suit. They were seated quickly at a quiet table, and they both ordered without having to look at the menu. Catherine told him about Mrs. Adolphi, and Victor listened attentively, his gaze a little too intense for her liking.

They managed to get through most of Catherine's Cobb salad and Victor's fish before he brought up the World Health Organization banquet a month away. "I was hoping we could go together," he said.

"Thank you, Victor. But I'm actually seeing someone, and he's going to be my date for the banquet."

Victor looked surprised. Very surprised. "I had no idea."

"He doesn't work here."

"I see. He must be a fascinating fellow for him to have caught your interest."

"He is," she said. "But I can't imagine there aren't a

dozen other women out there hoping you'll ask them to the banquet. I know you, Victor. You're a scoundrel."

"Is that really what you think?"

"I do. But it looks good on you. God—I'm sorry, but I've got to get going. Mrs. Adolphi stole my valuable email-checking time. And I believe it's my turn to spring for lunch, yes?"

"Fine," he said, although he didn't look happy about it. "If I'd remembered, I would have ordered something more expensive," he teased.

She smiled and put cash in the bill holder, then stood up, knowing Victor would, too. The guy had impeccable manners. He didn't need to know that she really wasn't in a rush to get back to work. She'd left her afternoon open in case the Security Council meeting ran long. She kissed him on each cheek, and said, "Next week, why don't we make reservations at Kurumazushi?" They both knew it was one of the most expensive restaurants in New York.

"All right, as long as we ask for separate checks," he said with a charming smile.

"Not a chance. See you later." She felt his gaze on her ass all the way across the room. When she arrived back at her office, she couldn't stop thinking about how she'd told Victor that she was seeing someone. Because she wasn't. Not really. The last thing she could ever ask Tony to do was go with her to the banquet. It wasn't even a matter of being seen together. He would hate it, she was sure. It was silly to consider it at all.

Although he'd surprised her the other night. She hadn't expected that luxury apartment or the posh furnishings.

She started reading an article, but realized she couldn't concentrate one iota. Whatever else happened between her and Tony Paladino, she had to stop thinking about him as often as she did. It was interfering with her life.

Just when her dreams were taking root and her life was falling into place.

Catherine sank back in her chair and sighed. But after that taste of what he was like in bed, what hope did she have?

FIVE MINUTES LATE, and Tony knew his mother was going to give him grief about it. Was it his fault there'd been an accident on Fifth Avenue? Besides, there was nothing urgent about this doctor's appointment. It was his dad's regular checkup, that was all. Tony was there to make sure his mom would get all the information straight. Either he or Luca, or sometimes Dom, accompanied her to each appointment.

Only, when he opened the door to the cardiologist's office, Dom was there. Sitting next to Mom, not talking. And Mom looked pissed.

"Tony. You came," she said. In the voice that used to make him break into a cold sweat when he was a kid.

"Accident on Fifth. I told you I'd be here."

"Well, your father's already in with the doctor. We'll just have to wait until he calls us in."

"That's fine," Tony said, taking a seat next to Theresa. She was wearing one of the dresses she reserved for church and important meetings. And she'd pinned up her salt-and-pepper hair, which, he knew, was her version of donning armor.

There were only two other people in the reception area, not including the women behind the desk. He opened his mouth, but before he said anything to his mother, he leaned forward to catch Dom's eye. "What are you doing here?"

"What, I can't be here when you are? I was worried about Pop, what do you think?"

"Yeah, okay." Tony wasn't about to engage in any of Dom's bullshit. "It's all going to be fine. We know that. This appointment is just a follow-up."

"I know that," his mother said, folding her arms over her black purse. The damn thing had been with her for so long he couldn't remember a time before it. It always reminded him of an old-fashioned doctor's bag. "I know a lot of things."

Here it was. The real reason she was giving Tony the evil eye. "What's that supposed to mean?"

His mother shrugged. God, she had that move down. It was okay, though. She was scared. She'd told him, when they were waiting for Joe to get out of surgery, that she felt guilty because she'd fed him terribly all those years. She should have given him plain food. Salads. More vegetables.

Tony let his anger drop like a used tissue. "Ma, just tell me what's wrong."

She turned to face him. "I have to hear from the neighbors you have a girlfriend? You can't tell me these things?"

He felt the beginning of a cold sweat. He was going to kill his brother. He leaned back this time, willing Dom to look his way. When he did, his brother held up both hands, his eyes agape as he shook his head.

"What are you talking about?" Tony said, keeping his cool. "What girlfriend?"

"Connie Busto said you were walking around with a woman. Just walking around, holding a box of cannoli like you were going to a picnic. I heard the same thing when I stopped by to see Father Zavala this morning. At church, I hear from Maryanne Di Vitis that you were holding hands. Holding your girlfriend's hand on a street where you know everyone! And I have to look like a fool because I know none of this."

"What…? She's a client. And we were not holding hands. I was showing her some porches the company had remodeled. There's no girlfriend. Holy Mother of God, this neighborhood is going to drive me insane. Why didn't you ask me about it?"

"I just did."

"Before you believed those vultures? All they care about is gossip. They're worse than the tabloids, and you fall for it hook, line and sinker, every time."

"I do not. When I heard that Dom told Felicia what's-her-name that she should jump off a bridge, I said he wouldn't say that. I know my boys."

"When did that happen?" Dom asked.

Theresa waved his question away. "What difference does it make? The point is I knew better."

"Ma—"

"Besides. Everyone said you were laughing. And happy." She was still frowning and darting looks at the door to the exam rooms. "You get that happy with all your clients?"

"Everyone, huh?"

"Never you mind. I don't remember you taking any other clients for strolls to show them porches."

"Ma—"

"So, this *client*. What's her name?"

Tony rubbed his eye. "Catherine Fox. Dad and I were talking about her restoration job the other day in the office."

"See, I knew you were talking business."

Tony just shook his head and sighed.

"You should bring her to dinner on Friday night."

"What?"

"If there's nothing for me to see, bring her. I'll tell you then if there's nothing to see."

"There's no way I'm bringing a client to dinner."

"Aha!"

"No, Tony," Dom said. "Mom's got a point. Bring her. She's new to the neighborhood, right? Maybe she wants to meet someone besides you and Sal."

Tony closed his eyes, not believing the words he was hearing. Not Dom's idiocy, because he was a complete jackass, but from his mother. Bring Catherine to a family dinner? Not a chance. God, he could just imagine the field day his family would have with her. Besides, it would send the wrong message. He wasn't about to take her to meet the folks.

After just one of his family dinners, she'd regret ever moving to Little Italy. His parents would treat her reasonably well; that wasn't what worried him. But Catherine would sure as hell find out what kind of neighbors she had. A bunch of gossips, especially the two old ladies on either side of her. There was nothing subtle about that pair. It wouldn't surprise him at all if they'd been snubbing her. But if she heard something they'd said from his mom and grandmother, she'd move out of that house so fast, it wouldn't be funny. At least she could flip it for a hell of a profit, but...

She'd also run from him. And he definitely didn't want that. In fact, he'd been thinking about her so often, it was getting a little out of hand.

Maybe it would be a good thing, letting her see what she was in for. She'd hold her own. She wasn't just beautiful; she had a striking presence, and she evidently read people as if they were open books.

But letting her see the truth could also break her heart. No. He wasn't going to ask her to dinner. Not now.

Not ever. The arrangement they had was great. He had no desire to rock the boat.

When he opened his eyes again, he cut the whole conversation off. "She's not my girlfriend. She's a client. Listen. As long as Dom's here, you gonna be okay if I take off? I've got work up to my eyeballs."

"You're leaving because maybe there is something between you and this client."

"I'm leaving because I have work to do." Tony kissed his mother's cheek, flipped Dom off behind her back and left the office, which was four blocks away from the UN complex. As he walked down the staircase, he dialed Catherine, which might not have been the best idea, but he didn't care.

"Tony."

"Hey, Catherine," he said. "I'm in the neighborhood. I know it's not lunchtime or anything, but I was thinking about that tour you were talking about."

"Now?"

"I knew it was a long shot. It's okay—"

"No. Now is fine," she said. "Give me ten minutes and I'll meet you at the visitor center."

9

CATHERINE'S HEART STARTED beating more quickly as she caught sight of Tony at the entrance. He'd already been through Security, so that made things simpler, and she knew just where she was going to take him. Nowhere out-of-bounds, of course. But he'd get a kick out of seeing the lobby of the General Assembly Building even if he couldn't see the hall. If there was time, she'd take him to the Secretariat Building, where her office was located, but that wasn't as impressive.

His smile, when he saw her, sent a shiver through her. Unfortunately, she'd have to keep her distance while he was here. Something she wished she'd thought of before seeing him in person, looking unforgivably hot in a sea-foam-green shirt that brought out the gold flecks in his eyes.

"Hey," he said, still smiling as they met in the middle of the busy floor.

Catherine held out her hand, and of course, he met the challenge flawlessly.

"Thank you for making time for me today," he said. "I don't want to steal you away from work, though."

"You aren't. But it can't be a full tour. Not this time. This is the best building to see, though, anyway."

He looked around, his gaze stopping for a moment on the soaring glass wall split into strips by gold pillars. Then, naturally, he looked up at a hanging artifact. "Is that...?"

"Sputnik. Well, a model of it. It goes with the rest of the fifties decor."

"I thought I was getting a *Mad Men* vibe."

"Follow me," she said, finding it difficult to blot out the image of him naked from her mind. The way his black trousers fit so perfectly made her want to slow down and walk behind him so she could enjoy the view. Lord help her, maybe this wasn't such a good idea. "I'll let you peek into the delegates' lounge. You'll love it. They refurbished everything—the chairs, the couches, the carpet. It's wonderful. I love to walk around the complex when I can, just enjoying the different buildings, with their international designs. We've got everything here. You could spend a whole week just checking out the amazing spaces without even setting foot inside the General Assembly Hall."

"You'll let me know when you have a free week?"

She laughed. "Come on."

"I probably should be better dressed. All these men are in suits and ties."

"You're fine. Better than fine. I'm a big fan of vintage shirts, especially in that shade of green."

"Thanks. Not that I'd admit this to just anyone, but I'm a big fan of the feel of silk."

"It's sinfully soft."

"So are you."

She blushed. But kept her tour-guide face on. She walked him around the sculptures and pictures that were liberally placed throughout the lobby. It was clear he found all of it as fascinating as she did.

Eventually, they made their way to the delegates' lounge, which wasn't a stop on any official tour. She wasn't even supposed to be in there, not without an invitation. She hoped she wouldn't run into her boss.

The coast was clear. After she'd finished pointing out the finer points of the restoration, she told Tony about her impromptu translation session between Mrs. Adolphi and the Russian designer.

"That's a real gift you have," he said. "Though I don't know if you speaking fluent Italian is going to do you any favors in the neighborhood."

"What do you mean?"

"Well, it depends on how thick your skin is, but sometimes it's better not to know what people are saying."

"I real—" Catherine spotted Victor and grabbed Tony's hand. She led him very quickly around the closest corner.

Tony glanced at their joined hands and she released him as if he'd scorched her. "What's wrong?" he asked.

"Nothing. I just saw someone I didn't want to talk to."

"A coworker?"

"In a manner of speaking, yes."

Tony leaned in close to her and lowered his voice. "I don't need to read people as well as you to know you're uncomfortable. I can leave right now, no problem."

"No. I mean, well, that would probably be best. Let's just make our way back to the visitors' entrance."

"Won't that be taking a chance you'll run into that person again?"

"I don't think so. Come on," she said, no longer holding his hand, but wishing she was. "I had lunch with him this afternoon and he asked me to go with him to a World Health Organization banquet. I know that he was honestly asking me for a date, and I don't want to change our relationship, so I sort of lied and told him I was going with someone else."

"Wait—is he the French guy?" Tony asked with a knowing smile. "Victor?"

She nodded. "How did you know?"

"I met him the other day, remember?"

"Oh, right." She shook her head. She'd forgotten all about Victor the moment she'd seen Tony. "I told him I was seeing someone. All I honestly wanted was for him to think I'm off the market. So don't worry. It has nothing to do with you."

Tony gave her a half grin that made her feel better instantly. "Let me tell you a little story," he said, and proceeded to recount his experience at the doctor's office as they walked to the elevator.

"Dom. That's his name. I keep forgetting that. You really believe he didn't tell your mom about us?"

"Yeah. I thought so at first, but he wouldn't do anything like that. He didn't need to, either. That simple walk we took has now basically become our engagement announcement. I warned you."

"They were pretty darn quick."

"Faster than the speed of sound. That's your neighborhood for you."

"I think I can handle it."

They were standing at the exit, and she got the idea that he didn't want to leave as much as she didn't want him to. If only she could have kissed him or something…

"I'll actually be seeing you very soon," she said.

"That's true."

"No pastries tonight. And I don't have anything for dinner, so eat before you come."

"Yes, ma'am."

She smiled and felt her cheeks get warm. "I'm sorry this couldn't have been a better tour."

"Best ever. Wouldn't trade it for the world."

She searched his eyes and wished, just for a moment, that they were more than what they were.

Tony stared right back, studying her face every bit as closely. "You know, if you wanted, you could come to a family dinner Friday night—"

Surprised, she blinked. "I'd love to. As long as it doesn't go too late, because I have to work Saturday morning."

He stopped. Raised his eyebrows. "Wait. You really want to come? After what I just told you?"

She nodded. "Clearly, you don't want me to go, though. So why did you ask?"

"Honestly?" he said. "I have no idea." He glanced around. "Look, it's not that I don't want you to meet them. I just don't want them to chase you away."

She thought about how it would be with her own parents. Oh, God. "That's it?"

"That's it," he repeated.

"Well, I wouldn't want to go if you'd be uncomfortable. But I am a client, so it might quell some rumors. And I've already met your father—" Her cell phone rang, and she took it out of her pocket. "This is Catherine Fox."

After hearing that she was needed back at her office, she put her boss on hold for a moment. "Sorry, I've got to go."

"Sure. Of course. I'll see you later," Tony said, looking a little shell-shocked.

Catherine hurried on her way, not just because she was needed, but because she was afraid he'd stop her and tell her he was just kidding about the family dinner. What she'd said was true, though. It might actually help matters for her to meet his family.

Or make things exponentially worse.

BY THE TIME Tony got to his mother's house he was in a state. It didn't help that he hadn't seen Catherine since he'd met her at the UN complex. A plumbing emergency in Queens involving a subcontractor had ruined Wednesday night, and something to do with her job had put the kibosh on Thursday. Not only was he frustrated that the two of them hadn't had sex again, he also hadn't been able to connect with her to lay down some groundwork for tonight's meal.

Of course, his mother had gone nuts the moment he'd told her Catherine was coming to dinner. From the condition the kitchen was in, he knew that she and his grandmother had been cooking everything they could think of, from *arancini* to *zeppole*. At least he'd had the good sense to bring the entire selection of wines that would go with each course. He deposited the heavy box on the hutch and went to look for the wine opener.

"Tony, help your brother set the table."

"Dom can set a table all by himself. He's a big boy now."

"Don't argue with me when I've got a big wooden spoon in my hand, young man."

"Young man," he said, joining his mother near the stove. All four burners were occupied, as were the double ovens. And there was the table, the big one they brought out when the extended family came over, bowing under the weight of…oh, God. "Who are you planning to feed with this, Ma? There's enough for the entire neighborhood here."

"What's left over you kids can take home. I'm sure

Catherine doesn't have anything decent in her refrigerator."

"Her refrigerator is tiny. She's in the middle of renovations. She doesn't have anywhere to put anything."

"So you boys all take extra, and bring her a little each time one of you goes to work at her house. See? Simple. Now go help your brother."

Tony just shook his head. No point in arguing. "I'm going to get the wine ready. Tell Luca to help."

"Luca's out back with your father at the grill."

"Of course you're making the *bistecca alla Fiorentina*." It was a huge cut of porterhouse steak, wood-grilled rare, and a show-off dish if there ever was one. They usually had it only on special occasions.

"Your father told me she's loaded. You want her to think we don't know good meat?"

"No, Ma. I don't want her to know you're nuts."

"Hey, watch your mouth."

He was still too fast for her. The spoon just missed his knuckles. "Where's Nonna?"

"Resting. She cooked all day."

"Nuts," Tony said under his breath as he went over to the box and pulled out the red wines. After he uncorked those, he put the already chilled whites in the patio fridge, which was, as always, full.

"Hey, Pop," he said, deeply inhaling the scent of the *Fiorentina*. He clapped his dad on the back and nodded at his brother. "So you're helping with the steak, huh? Interesting way to help."

Luca held up his half-empty glass of white wine. "I've had a tough day."

"Funny guy. I was with you for most of it. And no, I don't want to talk about it." They'd had trouble with a newer client who wanted to change things in her remodel after almost everything was finished.

"I like that you invited Ms. Fox to dinner," his father said. "She's nice. I was sorry I couldn't keep working with her. Not that I worry you aren't doing a good job. Just, she was nice. A little old-fashioned, I think."

"Only with her taste in restoration," Tony said.

"I'm not sure that's true. But what do I know." He looked at his watch. "She'll be here soon?"

"Yeah. Any minute. I heard about what the doctor said."

His father scowled and poked at the steak. "They're making a dinner fit for a king, and I've got to eat like a pauper. I ask you, what good is living a long life if I have to eat salad all the goddamn time?"

"You can eat other things. Just in moderation. And you know we all need you, so don't mess around. I'm still wet behind the ears. What would I do if I couldn't call you for advice every day?"

"Just what you're doing now," he said, then closed his eyes for a moment. "But I appreciate you asking all the same."

As Tony smiled, the doorbell rang. He hustled back into the house and went to get the door before Dom or, God forbid, his mother got it.

Catherine looked beautiful in a dress that was belted at the waist, with a pleated skirt that hit just below her knees. With the ballet slippers and her little sweater, she reminded him of pictures from the old scrapbook his mother kept.

"Welcome," he said, reminding himself that kissing was off the table for the night, "to my family home."

"It's a beautiful place," she said, stepping inside and glancing around. "It looks like—hmm."

"The house from *Moonstruck*, with Cher, right?"

"Yes. I guess I'm not the first to notice."

"They did some filming on this block," he said. "I suppose that big bouquet isn't for me?"

"No. But then I didn't know you were so fond of roses."

"My mother will love them. She's in the kitchen. Don't be surprised at the fuss she'll make, okay?"

"Remember," Catherine said, leaning close so no one would overhear, "I've lived in Italy. And I had Belaflore in my life. I'm well prepared."

It occurred to Tony that he never should have worried about prepping Cathcrine. He should have been worried about his family. "Good. They'll like you, anyway. Don't worry."

She walked with Tony into the formal dining room, the one they didn't use except for company. The table was set, despite Dom having to do it all by himself.

"Hello, Catherine," Dom said, giving her one of his most disarming smiles. Tony would have cared if she hadn't kept forgetting his name.

"Good to see you again—"

"Dom," Tony said. "Or Dominic."

The smile dimmed, and Tony wished Luca had been there to witness it.

"And this way is the kitchen," he said, mentally crossing his fingers that this whole thing wasn't the worst idea he'd ever had. His mother turned as they stood at the arched entrance. Her smile looked genuine, but her eyes were working overtime. He wasn't sure how she did it, but she could give a head-to-toe once-over to anyone at all without them having a clue.

"Catherine Fox, this is my mother, Theresa."

"It's a pleasure to meet you, Mrs. Paladino. The mo-

YOUR PARTICIPATION IS REQUESTED!

Dear Reader,

Since you are a lover of our books — we would like to get to know you!

Inside you will find a short Reader's Survey. Sharing your answers with us will help our editorial staff understand who you are and what activities you enjoy.

To thank you for your participation, we would like to send you 2 books and 2 gifts — **ABSOLUTELY FREE!**

Enjoy your gifts with our appreciation,

Pam Powers

SEE INSIDE FOR READER'S SURVEY

For Your Reading Pleasure...

We'll send you 2 books and 2 gifts
ABSOLUTELY FREE
just for completing our Reader's Survey!

YOURS FREE!
*We'll send you two fabulous surprise
gifts absolutely FREE, just for trying
our books!*

Visit us at:
www.ReaderService.com

YOUR READER'S SURVEY
"THANK YOU" FREE GIFTS INCLUDE:
- ▶ 2 FREE books
- ▶ 2 lovely surprise gifts

PLEASE FILL IN THE CIRCLES COMPLETELY TO RESPOND

1) What type of fiction books do you enjoy reading? (Check all that apply)
- ○ Suspense/Thrillers   ○ Action/Adventure   ○ Modern-day Romances
- ○ Historical Romance   ○ Humor   ○ Paranormal Romance

2) What attracted you most to the last fiction book you purchased on impulse?
- ○ The Title   ○ The Cover   ○ The Author   ○ The Story

3) What is usually the greatest influencer when you <u>plan</u> to buy a book?
- ○ Advertising   ○ Referral   ○ Book Review

4) How often do you access the internet?
- ○ Daily   ○ Weekly   ○ Monthly   ○ Rarely or never.

5) How many NEW paperback fiction novels have you purchased in the past 3 months?
- ○ 0 - 2   ○ 3 - 6   ○ 7 or more

YES! I have completed the Reader's Survey. Please send me the 2 FREE books and 2 FREE gifts (gifts are worth about $10) for which I qualify. I understand that I am under no obligation to purchase any books, as explained on the back of this card.

150/350 HDL GKEL

FIRST NAME	LAST NAME

ADDRESS

APT.#	CITY

STATE/PROV.	ZIP/POSTAL CODE

◀ If offer card is missing write to: Reader Service, P.O. Box 1867, Buffalo, NY 14240-1867 or visit www.ReaderService.com ▶

BUSINESS REPLY MAIL

FIRST-CLASS MAIL   PERMIT NO. 717   BUFFALO, NY

POSTAGE WILL BE PAID BY ADDRESSEE

READER SERVICE
PO BOX 1867
BUFFALO NY 14240-9952

NO POSTAGE
NECESSARY
IF MAILED
IN THE
UNITED STATES

ment I walked into your house I nearly swooned from all the delicious smells." Catherine walked over and held out the bouquet of roses—pink, white and yellow, a traditional favorite for happy occasions in Italy. "I wasn't sure what to bring, but I've always loved roses, and I hope you like them, too."

The smile that had looked genuine became genuine as his mother accepted the bouquet. Without turning at all, she said, "Tony, bring out the big vase."

He hesitated for only a second, but there was enough goodwill so far that he felt comfortable going down to the cellar and leaving Catherine on her own.

10

CATHERINE WAS A little worried about Tony's disappearance, but she tried not to let it show. Theresa was a fascinating woman. If Catherine wasn't a trained professional, she'd never have noticed Tony's mother checking out every inch of her. She'd thought long and hard about what to wear, and decided that a retro dress from the 1950s would be just the thing. Now that she'd seen the house—a throwback to a different era, with a velvet couch, flocked damask wallpaper and family photos on practically every surface available—she knew she'd chosen well.

"So, tell me, Ms. Fox, who recommended my husband's company to remodel your new home?"

"Practically everyone," she said. "And please, Catherine is fine."

"Okay, good. Everyone, huh?"

"I don't know if you knew the Calabrese family, but when I bought the place from them, they swore by Paladino & Sons."

"I knew them," she said, just as Tony arrived with a gigantic vase. "Do me a favor, Catherine. Stir the sauce while I put the flowers in water."

Catherine obeyed, of course, and stirred the rich ragout while Theresa fussed with the roses and told Tony to get another apron from the drawer.

He brought back what looked like a handmade red checkerboard apron that would cover her well. At first Catherine thought Tony was going to put the apron on her, but at the last second he realized his mistake and handed it to her.

"Joseph never told me how you knew the Calabrese family. I didn't think the house was even on the market."

"Belaflore, William and Carlotta's grandmother, was my nanny from the time I was six. She became my de facto grandmother and dear friend until she passed two years ago."

"I remember her name, but I only knew her children."

The tone, just shy of outright disapproval, gave Catherine every bit of information she needed.

"They wanted to move to Queens or New Jersey or something, but the father said no because they lived above their store." Theresa dried her hands with a lime-green towel while eyeing Catherine. "Are you keeping a store?"

"No, I'm not. At least I don't think so. Although I have to decide very soon or Sal's going to walk out on me and leave all his equipment behind."

"Sal's a good boy, but he gets impatient. He wants everything up front, like his mother. Which is good because if he took after his father, he'd be drunk half the time, and the other half an idiot."

"Ma," Tony said, "I've already warned Catherine about the rampant gossip around here. You're just proving my point."

"She's going to be a neighbor, right? So why shouldn't she know something about the people she's going to live with?"

Tony sighed. "I'll put the flowers in the dining room and take Catherine out to see Pop and Luca."

Catherine wasn't going to argue, but after she handed over the spoon, she said, "Whatever I can do to help, just let me know. My kitchen is all torn apart so I've been living off takeout. I can't thank you enough for inviting me to dinner. It's very kind of you."

"You're a client. And a neighbor." Theresa waved a hand. "Of course, you're welcome anytime."

Tony herded her out of the kitchen, dropped the roses off in a very large dining room and then led her to another door in the enormous house. She'd thought the front of the place had looked like every other brownstone in the older area, but now she was beginning to see that it was a single-family home, a lot like hers, in fact, but bigger. "This is all one unit?"

"Yep. Been in the family since my great-great-grandfather came over to work in America. He lived in a tenement for several years, but worked his way up to foreman in a construction company. He scrimped and saved and put every penny he could into real estate. The tradition has carried on."

"Which explains your place," she said, her voice low, so she wouldn't blow the facade. It was quite uncomfortable, not being free to touch him. To kiss him. And she gathered, by the way he yanked her into a bathroom, he felt the same.

He shut the door and then pulled her straight into a desperate kiss. She melted against him, the feel of his body soothing her nerves, although it didn't help her in the wanting-him department.

"Now I know why this wasn't a great idea," he whispered right before he kissed the line of her jaw, all the way up to the base of her ear.

"They say absence makes the heart grow fonder," she said, running her hands down his back.

"It also makes me harder, which isn't a good thing." He gave her one last kiss before stepping back. "Okay, we can't do this. Not here. Just dinner. Just a client. Nothing else."

"Except for the gossip."

"I warned you."

"It's okay. I'm glad I'm here, even though I'm frustrated, as well. How about tomorrow night we deal with this situation? Can you come to my place?"

"Just tell me when."

She had to kiss him one more time before they rejoined his family. "Let's go back. I'm looking forward to seeing your father again. And dinner. It really does smell amazing."

The kiss had ended too quickly, but it took him a minute to get his pants to lie straight. Then they went out onto a back patio that overlooked a small but lovely garden. There was Joe, the first Paladino she'd met. He opened his arms to her and gave her a hug.

"You look great," she said.

"That's supposed to be my line."

"I'm just glad you're feeling well. For what it's worth, your son Tony is doing a great job. I imagine almost as good as if you'd stayed with the project."

"For that, you can eat my dessert that I'm not allowed to have."

"Deal," she said rather quickly, and laughed along with Tony and his brother.

She shook Luca's hand and made a fuss over the steak, which was very familiar to her, even though she made sure not to let it show. They talked about the pleasant weather they'd been having, then Joe steered the conversation to the progress of her renovation, but the topic of business was swiftly shut down by his two sons. Soon it was time for dinner.

As they were seated, the true scope of the banquet became clear. "Are you planning on a second round of guests after we finish?" Catherine asked.

Everyone at the table, with the exception of Nonna, who looked as if she'd fit in on any side street in Tuscany, laughed.

"This," Tony said, "is all for us."

"You're a tiny thing," Theresa said, bringing out yet another dish.

"Don't let that fool you," Catherine said, earning her a smile of approval.

"Oh, great," Dom said. "I'm depending on a lot of leftovers."

"Is that a nice thing to say to our guest?" Theresa gave him the evil eye across the table.

"I love you, Ma," Dom volleyed, with a dazzling grin that made Catherine chuckle.

Joe rolled his eyes. Tony and Luca shook their heads.

Nonna just kept staring at Catherine. She tried her best to ignore the older woman's frown of suspicion, as if she was waiting for Catherine to stuff all the family silver into her purse.

CATHERINE WAS NOT only enjoying the food, she loved listening to the Paladinos talk, and watching the family dynamic. Theresa gave her the lowdown on where to shop for groceries, bread and wine near her home, and while she listened, she couldn't help but keep glancing at the three brothers.

All of them were very good-looking with their dark hair and eyes, but there were definitely differences among them. Luca wore his hair longer, pushed back. His eyes were large, and his aquiline nose gave him a great profile that made him look slightly bookish.

Dom could have stepped straight out of an Abercrombie & Fitch catalog. He had perfectly symmetrical features and a contagious smile. Of course, Tony's face was her favorite. Not to mention the rest of him. He took after his father in the eyebrow department, which she loved, and had a strong chin, a classic profile.

She lowered her gaze to her plate, having no idea what had been said while she'd been comparing the men. Theresa was still talking about where to get the best wine, so Catherine couldn't have been out of it for too long.

She took only a small portion of each dish, because she'd seen the table in the kitchen. After the first glass of prosecco was downed, the conversation got a lot livelier. Of course, most of the focus was on her, and she explained why she was so interested in art deco, answered more questions about her parents and then explained *again* why she wasn't going to flip the house.

Along with the third course, which was a small serving of angel hair pasta with wild onions, and yet another kind of wine, came the gossip. It was even thicker than the ragout. Word on the street was that Mrs. Whatever was having an affair with a man half her age, which was scandalous because she was the bookkeeper at the church. Also, another landmark building, one both Theresa and Joseph had visited all their lives, was being turned into a Ruth's Chris Steak House, which was deemed a desecration. It went on like this. Something terrible after something else terrible that would ruin everything.

It reminded her of the parties her parents had thrown. "You know, I really do think I'll fit in around here," she said. "I've attended scores of cocktail parties filled with dignitaries and celebrities and political leaders, and all they do is gossip. It's like the game of telephone. By the time the information would hit the wire services, the original message was garbled beyond belief, and far more salacious than when it had started."

The silence at the table let her know immediately that she'd had too much wine. She felt heat creeping up her neck and infusing her cheeks.

Theresa finally broke the silence. "We don't gossip in this house."

It didn't help at all that Tony and his brothers burst out laughing.

Their mother glared at them. "It's not gossip if it's true."

"Oh, no, I didn't mean to imply..." Catherine couldn't do a damn thing about the blush spreading across her face. She just smiled. "It's very kind of you to fill me in on the neighborhood. I haven't met many people. I know I'm an outsider, but I have great respect for the culture I'm moving into."

More silence.

This time Catherine kept her mouth shut.

Then Nonna finally spoke. In Tuscan Italian. "*Questa figa pensa che* she's going to get him to the altar."

Of course Catherine understood. Being called a scheming tramp wasn't exactly what she'd been hoping to hear from Tony's grandmother, but the woman looked to be a hundred. What she didn't know was if Tony had told the family she spoke the language, and it was only the grandmother who'd forgotten.

Or maybe there was another explanation—a not-so-friendly warning, perhaps?

TONY COUGHED TO cover his curse after his grandmother's comment. He hadn't heard every word, but he'd caught the gist. Not that Nonna was to blame. He hadn't remembered to tell the family that Catherine spoke Italian, and she'd mentioned only the UN official languages when she'd talked about her job.

Her diplomacy was front and center, as she asked his mother about a recipe, but all he wanted to do was grab Catherine and get her out of there. This had been the worst idea ever. He should have known. Hell, he had known, but he'd chosen to ignore the warnings all the same.

His appetite had vanished, so he just pushed his food around on his plate, polished off his wine and poured another glass. They still had the cheese course and dessert left.

He didn't jump at all when he felt Catherine's hand on his thigh. When he looked at her, she smiled. It was nothing like her smile when they were alone. What else would he expect? She was classy as hell, not like his... What did she even see in him? Was she slumming by hanging out with him?

He thought about the atmosphere at the UN. How easy it was to tell those who belonged there from the tourists.

"What was your favorite birthday dinner?" Catherine asked.

He'd clearly missed an entire conversation. But it didn't matter, as his brothers supplied the answer—in unison. "Fettuccine Alfredo, with chocolate ice cream and cannoli for dessert."

"My sons," Theresa said. "They love my cooking. And Nonna's, too, of course. Do you cook, Catherine?"

"A bit. I've always admired people who can, who have that gift. My mother worked when I was growing up, and she wasn't good in the kitchen. I picked up what I could over the years from Belaflore, our housekeepers and the occasional personal chef. But there's nothing in my small repertoire that comes close to what I've had tonight. I'm already full, but I can't seem to stop eating. Everything's simply too delicious."

His mother preened. One point in favor of the outsider. But it wasn't nearly enough. Tony didn't want to be angry at his family for being who they were. That wasn't fair. It didn't matter that he wasn't looking to get serious with Catherine. He liked her, respected her. But all his old-fashioned mother and her mother cared about was that she wasn't one of them.

"So, Luca," he said, "how's that new kid working out?"

"Gina's nephew? He's not thrilled about this golden opportunity, and it shows. Not that he's been a flake, just, he's got a band and he plays the guitar and that's in his head all the time. I heard them once, and they're not bad. But they're not the next big thing, either."

"Better he learns how to make a living than waste his time on useless dreams," Joe said. "A band. He expects to find a wife like that? What woman's going to want a guitar player for a husband?"

Luca shook his head. "He's still a teenager. He's not thinking about marriage yet."

"That's what's wrong with all of you young people." Joe looked at Catherine and waved his fork as he spoke. "None of them married. No grandchildren. By Dom's age, I was already with their mother. Did I complain that I had to be an apprentice to my father? Never."

Catherine ever-so-wisely put a big piece of steak in her mouth as she nodded sympathetically.

"You wanted to be like your father," Theresa said, "and you still complained. Tony, come help me with the cheese, huh?"

He hated leaving Catherine alone, but the summons

wasn't negotiable. "Sure, Ma." It also wasn't about the cheese.

She took him past the table where the cheese course was set out on a big platter, all the way to the basement door. "I told you something was up with her."

"What?"

"Only a client? I don't think so. The way she looks at you isn't just being a client."

"I'm not going to talk to you about this."

"Okay, fine. But you be careful, huh? She's smart, this one. She'll have you wrapped around her finger before you even know what's what. Take my word for it." Theresa touched the side of her nose with her index finger. "I'm not wrong about this."

"Do you want me to take the cheese to the table?"

The stare she gave him meant he'd hear more about it later. When the outsider was gone. He didn't care. The sooner this stupid night was over, the better.

"I have to clear some of the table first."

"I'll give you a hand," he said, grateful for the distraction.

She shrugged. "Do what you like. That's all you do, anyway," his mother said, and walked out.

He heard Catherine offer to help, which was the third time tonight. Like the other times, she was turned down.

Could he even go back out there and be pleasant? None of this should have been a surprise. But he hadn't realized how much he wanted his family to see Catherine as someone special. So maybe he was getting a little serious about her. Hell, he didn't know.

Stupido.

But he'd go back, finish the meal. Make conversation. And hope that when the night was over, she didn't tell him to get lost.

11

"I'M SORRY," TONY said the minute they'd left the house and were on the street.

"What for?" Catherine studied his expression, but as usual she was having difficulty reading him. Of course she realized his apology had something to do with the evening, but there were quite a few things he could mean.

"I should have realized it would be uncomfortable for you. My grandmother didn't mean to be rude. I neglected to tell them you spoke Italian. Not that it would've excused what she said. I just wanted you to know she wouldn't have deliberately tried to hurt your feelings."

"It's fine. Truly, I don't mind. I've hardly met anyone from the neighborhood yet. But tonight was a good beginning. And I like your family."

"Why? My parents are living in a past that never really existed. It's as if they're stuck in a time warp. It's not just them, either. All the old-timers, they want everything to be the way they remember, but their memories are fairy tales."

"Wow," she said, walking toward the subway. "I think you had a much worse time than I did."

He shifted the heavy bag of leftovers to his other arm.

"Where are you planning on keeping this food? You'd have to buy a whole new fridge."

She latched on to the change of subject eagerly. "I was hoping you'd take it to your place, then bring some of it tomorrow night."

"Ah. About that."

She slowed, not liking the hesitation in his voice one bit. "What is it?"

"I know dinner ran late. But I'd like it if we could be together tonight."

The tension eased out of her shoulders. "Well, I suppose that would mean going to your place because of the food, but I'd have to get up super early to go back to mine before work in the morning."

"You're right. It's stupid."

She started walking more quickly. "Not stupid. In fact, I have an idea. Why don't we get a cab, which will take me by the house to gather my things, then we'll go to your place. As long as Dominic isn't planning to make a surprise visit."

"Dominic knows if he does that again he'll be banished forever. No worries."

"Good," she said, waiting for the cloud that was hanging over him to lighten. But it didn't. "Are you sure about this?"

"Yeah. Why do you ask?"

"You puzzle me. I can't tell if you were truly bothered by your family, or if you're upset because you think I was bothered."

He hung his head, but just for a second. "Let's find a cab at the corner. And if you don't mind, let's not talk any more about my family tonight."

"Deal," she said, and hurried along with him to the cross street.

IT WAS A quarter to ten by the time they reached Tony's place. She was pleased that despite his subdued mood he still wanted her to spend the night with him. It took them forever to put the food away, but only because Tony couldn't seem to keep his hands off her.

"Okay, I think that's it," she said, closing the fridge door and turning just as he caught her around the waist.

"I wasn't finished."

"With what?" she asked, all innocence, his hungry look and low raspy voice exciting her.

"Kissing you," he said, pulling her close. The way he took her mouth, possessive and demanding, accelerated more than her heartbeat. She wrapped her arms around his neck, and he thrust his tongue between her lips as if he meant to stake his claim.

It was thrilling. Her breasts brushed against his chest, her hardened nipples sensitive enough to make her breath catch. She squeezed her legs together as tightly as she could, needing the pressure, wanting so much more.

His hands tightened on her waist, and he lifted her up onto the center island. Their eyes were level now, and she could see the black of his widening pupils.

"Christ, you're beautiful," he whispered, then kissed her as he slid his hands underneath her dress, moving them up her thighs, which seemed to part of their own volition. "I've been thinking about this since the last time you were here," he said. "Except this time, I intend to finish what I start."

She pulled back, needing to breathe for a moment. The way he skimmed his fingers in circles between her legs, knowing what he planned to do, threatened to make her hyperventilate.

He let her mouth go and studied her for a long moment as one of his hands slid up to her hip.

"What's this?"

"Panties."

"Really?"

"A different kind."

"Have I ever told you how much I like the way you think outside the box?"

"What a lovely way to say I've got a thing for fancy underwear."

"Yeah," he said. "That, too."

She bit on her lower lip as he studied her undergarments by touch alone. In the meantime, though, she unbuttoned his shirt, stopping when she reached his pants. She ran her hands over his chest. She liked that he had the perfect amount of chest hair. She'd never been a big fan of shaved chests. Besides, the hair was soft and his flat nipples stood out.

"Can you wait just a second?" he asked, his voice lower still.

"Why?"

"Reconnaissance mission."

She'd barely nodded when he lifted the skirt of her dress.

"You do like to make me work for it, don't you?" he said with a grunt.

"Not my intention, but it's kind of hot, watching you solve this puzzle."

"I was going to go caveman style and rip them off, but they look so pretty I think I'd rather watch you take off the dress."

"Huh," she said, feeling her blush, but not minding it. "Sounds as though you might have a thing for fancy underwear, too."

"Not until you I didn't."

"Don't tell me you haven't been turned on by ladies

in their intimate wear," Catherine said with a seductive smile.

"I have. But not like this. Tell you what. I'm going to switch gears."

"How?"

"Just relax. It'll be fine."

His teasing fingers slid down her thighs until he was outside the dress. As he leaned in to kiss her again, this time softly, just lips brushing lips, those same fingers moved to the buttons on the top part of her dress. She actually had to chase after his mouth when he leaned back.

He pushed open the bodice, his eyes darkening as he caught a glimpse of her bra. It was the same silk as her panties, white, with lace on the sides and straps. It was one of her favorite sets, and she'd debated wearing them with garters and stockings, but she'd finally decided to go without. Now, she was sorry. It would have felt wonderful to have him remove them.

His hands went to her breasts, the cups that almost hid her nipples. It was obvious that she was aroused, but that was nothing compared to the havoc he caused when he bent down and sucked her right nipple into his mouth, silk and all.

She moaned at the feeling of his hot breath, the way he wetted the material. She'd always had sensitive nipples, but her body was going into overdrive.

She shivered when he moaned with her in his mouth. She tried to wrap her leg around his hips, but the way he was bent made it impossible. "I'm having trouble sitting still."

"Mmm. Wiggle some more. I like it." He gave her other breast equal attention. She touched the wet spot over the breast he'd just left, sliding the material across and around her ever hardening bud.

"Well, shit," he said, standing up straight. "I can't..." He took hold of her and lifted her, making it easy for her to wrap her legs around his waist, loop her arms around his neck. She got busy as he walked, nuzzling that strong jaw of his all the way through the apartment until he reached the master suite.

He put her down next to the bed, kissing her quickly before he pulled down the comforter. Then he walked backward several paces. "Please," he said.

It was exciting, taking her dress off for him. She did it slowly, starting with the belt. "I think me taking off my dress means you need to get down to your underwear, too."

"I'm not wearing anything special."

"Doesn't mean I won't like it," she said, teasing him by lifting up her skirt partway—just enough to give him a glimpse of the white lace at the bottom of her satin tap pants.

His cock jumped enough for her to see it through his trousers.

"Come on," she said, gyrating her hips while she rubbed the still-damp silk over her nipples. That she felt sexy as sin in her La Perla high-wasted culotte and matching bra, despite the fact that they hadn't turned off the lights, made her bolder. As did his dark eyes, his rapid breathing and the sound of his zipper going down. The best part, though, was the visual connection between them. It was so intense she refused to blink.

He dropped his pants, and yes, he'd worn navy boxer briefs. She liked them very much, and let him know by pulling her dress up and off, letting it puddle on the floor. He let his shirt fall, leaning forward as if his body was ready to mutiny and take her as she stood.

"My God," he whispered.

"I love it when your voice gets all smoky."

"You do, huh?"

She nodded. "And when you narrow your eyes like you've got some big master plan going on inside that head of yours."

"Only one thing going on up there," he said with a husky laugh, his gaze roaming the front of her. "I've never seen anything like that."

"Really? That makes it extra nice." She held her arms out, and when she figured he'd looked his fill, she turned around, giving him a view of her behind while she reached back and unclasped her bra.

She heard his sharp inhale when she let the bra slip from her shoulders. Then, in a very Vargas pinup girl move, she looked at him over her shoulder and raised a fingertip to her lips.

"Fuck," he murmured, although she doubted he realized he'd said it aloud.

"I'm glad you like it."

"I like everything, except the fact you're too far away."

She turned back and glanced at the prominent bulge in his boxer briefs. She carefully put her fingers underneath the high waist of her panties, cocked her head as she waited for him to do the same with his briefs, then, smiling broadly, said, "One, two, three, go." And she stripped off her bottoms, kicked off her shoes and dived under the sheet.

He was still struggling with his socks, cursing again in colorful language, until he finally crawled in next to her.

When they were skin to skin, all the way from her chest to her knees, she sighed and moaned at the same time. But that was okay, because he sounded like a man who'd just found heaven.

"The great thing about our arrangement," she said,

her eyelids drifting closed as he nibbled on her neck, "is that we can do anything we want."

"Uh-huh," he said, moving his teasing to her jaw. "Wait, what do you mean?"

"Well, that we're…you know. Not serious. It's like permission. We know it's only for fun. No dire consequences if something isn't perfect."

He moved his head back and looked at her. "Are you suggesting sex with you could be anything but perfect?"

"That's sweet, but yes. I'm not saying it's not going to be perfect, but if it isn't, so what?"

Tony stole her breath away with another searing kiss, and when they finally took a much-needed breath, he whispered, "I love the way you think."

12

ALTHOUGH HE'D KISSED that imperfect idea off her lips, Tony actually agreed with her. It was freeing to have no expectations. Though he had that with Rita, and this was definitely not that.

He wasn't sure why it felt different, though.

But he refused to think about it now. Not while he had this beautiful woman in his arms. In fact…

He rolled her gently onto her back, kissed her lips, her delicate jaw, the curve of her neck, then the hollow. All the while, he explored her silken skin. Her nipples were hard like pebbles, and when he squeezed one between his index finger and thumb, her reaction told him a lot. He hadn't squeezed hard, but he was glad to know she was open to exploration.

All the women he'd been with before and after Angie had welcomed a little bit of daring. He wasn't sure why he'd thought Catherine might be the exception, but it was true. Probably because she was so different from anyone he'd ever been with. Certainly more elegant, more worldly.

Her hands, both of them, were in his hair. Not exactly pushing him lower, but there was definitely a suggestion that she wouldn't mind. Far be it from him to question her wishes.

When he lapped at her left nipple, she tugged on his hair in a way that let him know she liked what he was doing. Her moan helped with that, too.

He circled the little bud, and sucked it between his lips. With nothing between him and her skin, she tasted amazing, and it finally dawned on him that she smelled like roses.

Her leg got into the game, pressing against his butt with her calf. It caused his cock to rub against her upper thigh, not quite on the mark, but close.

"Oh," she said, letting her breath carry the word away. He used his free hand to move down her side, then over to the smooth flesh of her belly.

His reward was a jerk of her hips. There had been a plan, a good one, to take his time and move down her body until he'd memorized everything, but that jerk put a kink in the works.

Instead of the slow stroll, he more or less sped down to just above her delicately trimmed V. The scent of her was stronger here. Pulling at him like a Siren's call.

He looked up at her, and her beautiful blue eyes were half-lidded and dark, her lips parted and the tips of her teeth running over the place he wanted to kiss almost as much as he wanted to explore where he was.

Without losing eye contact, he parted her thighs, lifted her legs and eased them over his shoulders. Then he tore his gaze from hers and used his thumbs to reveal her moist, pink heat.

The first swipe of his tongue made him moan and his cock jerk impatiently. Tough. He tasted the sea and the essence of woman, beguiling and addictive. A few more long strokes all the way up to her clit, and then he circled the bud peeking out from her hood. Her legs on his back trembled. Catherine groaned and tugged on his hair. It didn't hurt. There was nothing but pleasure running through him.

As he learned what she liked best—slow pressed circles, quick flicks, teasing on the outer perimeter—he reacted. She'd urge him to focus, to flick and circle.

Her trembling increased, as did her cries, and with one final tug on his hair, she let go, jerking hard enough to unbalance him as her orgasm swept over her like a high tide.

He zeroed back in.

"Tony," she said, her voice mostly breath.

He looked up.

"I'd really like it a lot if you put on a condom right now and shagged me into the mattress."

"Yes," he said, trying hard not to immediately come, with no direct stimulation at all. "Yes, I can do that." He somehow got his knees beneath him and bent over far enough to grab a condom. "And for the record, you speaking Euro is very hot. *Shagging* is a great word."

"You think so?" she said, an aftershock making the last word shaky.

He nodded as he quickly rolled the condom down his cock. "I do. And I'd like to say, also for the record, that I had planned to take my time with you, to give you every pleasure possible, but now that you've asked me so nicely, I'm probably not going to last much longer than I did before."

"I don't mind. In fact, I'll make it easier for both of us."

He didn't understand what that meant until she leaned back against the pillows, pulled one leg off his shoulder until her foot was on the bed, and spread the other leg wider. With a wicked smile that looked incredibly hot on her angelic face, she reached down with her right hand and spread herself for him. "I'm thinking that if you stop ogling now, we'll probably come at the exact same time."

"You think I can touch your body and not come instantly?"

She inhaled raggedly for a few beats before meeting his gaze. "I believe in you. You're a strong, capable man. I think you can take us both to the moon and back."

He closed his eyes and sent up a quick prayer that he wouldn't embarrass himself completely, then willed his cock to settle the hell down. The moon? No sweat. Since he was already on his knees, he stole a quick kiss before maneuvering into position, all while not daring to look at what her fingers were doing. Or even glance in that area.

As ready as he was going to get, he squared himself into firing range, and after a quick tug on his balls, went for it. All the way in one stroke.

He didn't come, although a heart attack wasn't out of the question. Hearing her gasp made him insane, and God, he could feel her hand moving under him. There was no need to look down; he could imagine everything with perfect clarity, all while looking into her half-closed eyes, just the rim of blue iris visible around her pupils.

Pulling out slowly, until the tip of his cock was between her warm, wet lips, he pushed hard again, moving the bed, her body, the whole damn building. Her mouth had opened as if in a scream, but there was no sound outside of a kind of squeak, which somehow turned him on even more. How was that even possible?

"You're so…"

"What?" she asked. "I'm so what?"

"Amazing."

"You've said that before."

"Astonishing."

"Yes," she said. "Better."

"You like that?" he said, pulling out inch by inch.

"I like it when you talk to me. When you say nice things. Or dirty things. Either is fine."

His head dropped again, for longer this time. "You're going to kill me."

"No. Don't die. Not until we come. Together. Synchronized orgasms."

He laughed, groaned. "I don't think I can wait."

"It won't be long. I'm already having to slow it down."

"Slow it—?"

"My finger. The second time tends to come faster."

He choked on a laugh, because there was no way he could form a word. But somehow he managed to thrust into her again. He had to freeze there, with his cock buried, on the brink, the knuckles of her right hand rubbing against his body in a circle that was gaining momentum.

"Again," she said.

"So fucking hot," he murmured, his voice a mere croak.

"For me, too," she said. "Now you need to stop screwing around and just do it. Hard. Okay?"

He very nearly lost it right then, but the woman wanted it fast and hard, and he was not going to disappoint her. "Who are you?" he said, as he pulled back so fast he slipped out all the way. It didn't take but a second to get back on track. "And where is that prim and proper beauty in that black skirt?"

"It's still me. Free to ask for what I want," she said, through several deep gasps. "All because of you."

"Me?"

"You make me brave, Paladino. You make me wanton."

Her words spurred him into a brutal pace, sweat beading on his hairline, his heart beating its way out of his chest. He'd never heard that word spoken before. "Wanton," he repeated. It was like hearing he was a sex god.

After hoping with all his heart that he hadn't said that last bit out loud, he couldn't think anymore. Not while he was having his mind and body shredded into atoms. He couldn't see. Could barely breathe. Wanted it to last forever, knowing full well he wouldn't survive.

"Now," she cried. "Nnn-n-n—"

He broke. He was in to the hilt and coming like he'd empty his whole being inside her. Feeling her squeeze the entire length of his shaft as she trembled underneath and around him.

It took a couple lifetimes for his own body to stop shaking. With all the strength of a newborn kitten, he somehow managed to fall beside her on the bed, their bodies still touching.

CATHERINE STARED UP at the ceiling. She could see it perfectly well because they still hadn't turned off any lights. Another way being with Tony was unique.

So was asking him to talk dirty to her. And then telling him when to wrap things up.

She smiled a little at that. It was the opposite of what she did in bed. With a partner. She'd always liked the idea of asking for exactly what she wanted. Which should not have been a difficult thing to do.

Yet it had been, until Tony came along. "You know what's interesting?"

A burst of laughter came from Tony. "What would that be?" he said, and she could hear the grin in his voice.

"I would have thought that you, being from such a traditional Italian family, would have had more difficulty with me taking over the...game plan."

After a bit of groping, he found her hand and squeezed

it. "I guess we surprised each other. Because I wouldn't have thought that you'd be the type to be so bold."

She turned her head and found him looking at her, the laugh lines by his eyes making him look younger somehow. Certainly more handsome. "I know. Why do you think that is?"

He held up a hand. "One sec." He turned away from her for a moment, grabbed some tissues, then pulled up the comforter so they wouldn't get cold now that the high was wearing off.

She took advantage of the mini break and sipped some much needed water from a bottle that had been left on the nightstand. By the time they were both back in position she was relieved that the cozy intimacy was still intact. It got even better when he found her hand again.

"I think," he said, "that we click in a way that's unusual."

"Explain?"

"From an objective standpoint, you're completely out of my league."

"I am not."

"Yeah, you are. I'm not putting myself down. But you have to admit we come from different worlds."

"Okay, I'll give you that. But you're certainly not from the wrong side of the tracks, and I'm not going to be handed the keys to an empire."

"My point is there's so much I like about you. We have a lot in common. Your taste, your willingness to take on a challenge. The work you do. You could have gone a whole different way, but you're very independent for a person who's had the kind of life you've led. I'm the kind of guy who knew from the beginning what I was going to do, who I'd be."

"Also admirable, but how does that make us unusual?"

"It's not a negative thing at all. I'm really glad we're getting to know each other, in all kinds of ways. But we both know your family would have a fit if we ever really got together, and, well…"

"I'm not Italian. Or Catholic."

He nodded. "I'm not saying either of us allows our families to run our lives, but that doesn't change the fact that we're…improbable, and I believe it makes us brave."

"How is that different from what I said?"

He shook his head. "I'm with you because I like you, and I think it's great that we feel comfortable enough to step outside our comfort zones. Not just in bed, either. You do realize I don't usually pitch in on jobs like I'm doing with you."

"I didn't think so. And I'm not exactly the DIY type of person."

"But the sex part is also sensational, so…"

She grinned. "Don't tell me you're ready…"

"I wish." He slid deeper under the covers, running a hand down her pale skin. "But soon."

She shimmied down until they were pressed against each other, her leg entwined with his. The feel of her made him wish he was a teenager again. Her hand was suddenly on his ass, giving him a little squeeze, and it wouldn't surprise him at all if he rose to the occasion sooner than he thought he could.

13

THE FOLLOWING FRIDAY, Tony had just finished a walk-through with a new client. The building was in China-town, five stories, with a commercial property on the ground floor and apartments above. The new owners, a group of young real estate flippers based in Connecti-cut, wanted him to make the top four floors into high-end condos and redo the commercial space so they could charge four times the rent. But they were hagglers, new to Paladino & Sons, and Tony's big decision was whether the money was worth the annoyance he and his crews would have to put up with.

They left the building and stood on the street, five young hotshots ready to become the next "real estate moguls," and him with his touch-pad spreadsheet and enough impatience to walk away if they called them-selves that one more time.

"Look, I'll send you a bid. If you like it, fine. If not, that's fine, too."

"You do know this could be the first of many jobs for your family operation," said the shortest one with the four-hundred-dollar haircut and enough attitude to fill Madison Square Garden.

"It's possible," he said slowly, watching their smug expressions dim. "We're booked through next year, but maybe I could bring in a few more subcontractors."

"We don't want the shit end of the work pool."

"No one who subcontracts for us is second best. It's hard as hell to be on our wait list."

"Mambo Italiano" rang out from his cell phone, and he had no compunctions about leaving the party with a quick, "Anything else?" He gave them a few seconds to respond. When no one did, he smiled. "I'll get the bid to you next week," he said, before he crossed the street and answered the phone. "Catherine?"

"Am I interrupting?"

"Not at all. In fact, I was just going to call you."

"Oh." The smile in her voice made him smile along with her. "You go first."

"What are you doing this weekend?"

"Uh, working on the house."

"Can I get you to change your mind?"

"Depends." She laughed. "Yes, of course. Tell me what you're thinking."

He started walking again, a definite lift in his step. "I'd like you to pack a bag for an overnight stay, and be ready to go early tomorrow morning. Around eight. Casual clothes. Plus something nice, just in case."

"Wait a minute. You can't— You have to tell me more than that."

"Why? Don't you trust me?"

Her silence lasted long enough to give him second thoughts. "I'm not actually that good with surprises."

"Okay," he said, disappointed, but anxious for her to just say yes. He was already looking forward to getting out of the city, away from his family, her work, his work. "I'm—"

"No, stop. You don't have to tell me anything."

"You sure?"

"Yes," she said softly. "I do trust you, Tony."

He'd been teasing. The trip would be their first real time to get away from the strictures of pretense, the hiding and the nonsense from the neighbors. It had little to do with trust. But something about the quietly spoken words got to him. "You won't be sorry."

"I already know that." Her smile was back. "So, I'll be ready by eight."

"Perfect. Wish I could see you tonight, but, well, I've got my cousin's thing and—"

"I know. But it'll give me a chance to look at some wallpaper and get to sleep at a good hour."

"We're all set, then." He saw his next appointment, Mr. Diamond, standing outside his store a few doors away. "How about we meet at the Canal Street subway at Broadway?"

"Perfect. I can't wait," she said.

"Me, neither." As soon as they disconnected, he realized she hadn't told him why she'd called.

TONY GOT TO the subway entrance early. He hated that he couldn't pick her up at her place, but it would defeat the purpose of sneaking away if everyone saw them walking together, her with an overnight bag in hand. Nothing was going to spoil this trip. Having her all to himself, no distractions, no Dom barging in. Tony still hadn't gotten over that one.

He saw her walking up the stairs and he raced down to meet her, taking her suitcase before he gave her a quick kiss. For some reason he hadn't expected her to wear jeans, a T-shirt and a light jacket, even though it was perfect attire for what promised to be a warm spring day.

"You're early," she said.

"So are you. Come on," he said, touching the small of her back. "It's only a short walk."

"We're staying in SoHo?"

"Not even close. But we are making a quick stop before we head out."

The Park-It was only a block away, and he was a little too excited to show her the car he'd borrowed for the trip.

"You own a cherry-red Mustang?"

"No, but I did make a friend who would let me borrow his."

She grinned. "How clever of you."

"Always thinking ahead." When he popped the trunk, he almost pointed out the elaborate sound system mounted in the trunk, but he held back.

Once they were both settled inside the car, he was ready to head straight for the I-95, but Catherine wanted coffee and that sounded like a great idea. They hit the first coffee place they saw, but she had to go in while he double parked. Having a car in New York sucked. But soon enough they were on their way out of the city.

"Are you going to tell me where we're going?"

"Nope."

"Okay, what if I guess?"

"I'll tell you the truth if you get it right."

"Can I ask questions?"

"Sure you can."

She stared at him for a long moment and then laughed. "I can ask but you won't answer."

Tony just smiled.

Catherine turned in her seat, so she was looking more at him than the road ahead. "Will you tell me if I'm hot or cold?"

"You're always hot."

"Good answer. Is it an hour away?"

"Cold."

"Half an hour?" she asked, her voice as innocent as a child's, but he was onto her.

"Colder, and no you can't go through every time on the clock."

"Not fair," she said, and pouted just enough to make him want to kiss her.

"You're right. Let's get creative. After we get to the interstate, all right?"

"Absolutely. Which interstate?"

"I-95."

She was quiet, and he looked over to find her frowning. "That's not helpful at all. I have no idea where that goes."

Tony smiled. This was the best idea he'd had in years. Except for a brand-new idea that popped into his head. There was a gas station up ahead, and he turned into it but didn't park by the pumps. Instead, he stopped the car at the far end of the lot, where they could have some privacy.

"Is something wrong with the car?"

He undid his seat belt and turned to her. "What's wrong is that I haven't had a single real kiss. That's not going to work."

"I couldn't agree more," she said, her voice turning to a whisper as he cupped her neck and brushed his thumb over her cheekbone.

She met him halfway and the moment he touched her lips with his own he felt better. He hadn't felt stressed, yet muscles relaxed all the way down his back.

A single touch of her tongue on his lower lip changed the soft caress into something wilder, although he couldn't forget where they were. But just because it had to be brief didn't mean it wasn't great. It thrilled him, as always, when he heard her pleasure in a whimper, when she ran her fingers through the back of his hair.

A horn honked, breaking the mood very effectively, but when he turned to look at the bastard who'd interrupted, he saw it wasn't about them at all.

"Better?" she asked.

"Much. Need anything before we continue?"

"I don't know," she said, pausing, a mischievous gleam in her eye. "Do I?"

Tony laughed. "Very sneaky. Good to know that about you early in the—" His brain shorted. He'd almost said *relationship*. This was it for them. Several stolen weeks, maybe even months, but that was all he could see for them. There was still a very good chance Catherine wouldn't stick around. Damn, he hoped he hadn't spooked her.

But no, she just looked at him, her lips curving up in a beautiful, soft smile.

BY THE TIME they hit the interstate, Catherine had finished her coffee and had talked more about her work, and what it had taken to get assigned to the New York office. It was so easy with Tony. His interest was real, which made a huge difference, and she shared his enthusiasm to use their time in the car to get to know all kinds of safe things about each other. Like his most memorable vacations and what sports he'd played in high school. She loved every second of it, but she hadn't forgotten his earlier suggestion about getting creative.

"Okay," she said, "I think we should do what you suggested and stop talking about such ordinary things."

"I did say that, didn't I?" He gave her a look she thought was him making a decision, but as usual, she wasn't 100 percent sure.

"How about," he said, "some truth or dare?"

"Really? The kids' game?"

"It's only a kids' game if children are playing."

"Ah, but I don't have much in the way of illicit secrets."

He reached over the console and took her hand in his. "I don't care if they're illicit. I just want to use this time wisely. You fascinate me, Ms. Fox."

"So, shouldn't we just be playing truth?"

His laugh made her warm inside. "Okay. Truth it is. You get the first question."

"Brave boy. Um, give me a second. There are a lot of things I want to ask." She squeezed his hand, and got more courageous when he squeezed back. "Okay. Why didn't you and your ex have kids?"

He coughed. "Whoa. You don't mess around."

"If it's too personal—"

"It's not," he said. "We agreed. Truth. I wanted children right away, but Angie didn't. She wanted to pursue other interests before becoming a mom."

"Other interests?"

"She tried her hand at a few things. Writing. Painting. But she ended up becoming a personal chef in Tribeca. She and a friend from writing class went into business together. It's pretty successful, considering the competition."

"Wow, good for her. Does she specialize in Italian cooking?"

"Nope. Healthy eating. She knows every diet plan in the world, so it suits her. Besides, I think it was her way of thumbing her nose at my mother, who never let her forget she wasn't the best Italian cook."

"Interesting," Catherine said. "And you didn't mind putting off the children?"

"Not at all. And I didn't care if she wanted to work after we had kids. Although my attitude didn't go over very big with her family. Or mine. You've seen they live in a time warp."

"I'm getting that, more and more. Although it seems your generation is quite different."

"Yeah. I agree. But that's been a mixed blessing. A lot of the people I went to school with have moved out. Mostly to Jersey or Queens, but I know a number of people who moved out of state. Even Dominic wants to move uptown. Get away from the old neighborhood. He's pretty determined to see how far his wings can spread."

"Modeling?"

"Nah. He uses his looks, but he wouldn't want that to be the basis of his success. And I believe it's way past my turn."

"Shoot."

He changed lanes, then settled in again, still holding on to her hand. "Why aren't you married?"

"What kind of a question is that?"

"One I don't know the answer to. You're gorgeous, smart, confident, engaging. I can't imagine men aren't lining up. That guy who wants to take you to that dinner, for example. He's exactly the kind of man I imagine you with. Not some blue-collar contractor like me."

Catherine studied him, taken aback not just by his description of her, but by his perception of himself. "I can say the exact same thing about you."

"You kind of already did the other night."

"Oh." She remembered. Not quite the same, but okay. "Anyway, I'm not married because I haven't been with anyone I loved enough."

"But you've been in love?"

"That's a new question, and I get to ask mine next."

"Right, yes," he said. "Go for it. This is pretty interesting."

"How old were you the first time you had sex?"

He laughed. "I didn't see that one coming, either. I was fifteen. She was seventeen."

Catherine turned just a little bit more, wanting to see as much of his face as she could. "What's the age of consent in New York?"

"We were both within the law."

"Were you nervous?"

"Of course. I was fifteen. She was hot, and she made me swear to God I wouldn't tell anyone. And believe me, at that age, keeping that secret was far more difficult than it sounds. I think you're the first person I've told."

"No. What about your brothers?"

"I wouldn't have trusted them with something like that. Besides, they were just kids."

"Huh. Was it a one-time thing or did you keep seeing her?"

"Hold up, Sherlock," he said, raising his brows at her. "I think you're way over the question limit."

"I know, but it's so much fun."

"Well, let's see how much fun it is when you're answering the same question."

"God, I was eighteen. I didn't have great feelings about the guy I was with, I just didn't want to be a virgin anymore."

"Who was he?"

"He was studying math at Howard while I was getting my undergraduate work done at Georgetown. We were at a party together, and we went back to my dorm room and did the deed."

"And?"

She rolled her eyes, not loving this particular question, but her quest to find out everything about Tony required some give to her take. "The earth didn't move. It was over fast, he was a lousy kisser and we never saw each other again."

"Romantic."

"I'm sure you were a regular Don Juan your first time."

He didn't quite roll his eyes, but she got the gist. "On the plus side, I was raring to go again ten minutes later."

"That's a big plus."

"Except her parents came home and I sprained my ankle jumping out of her window while making my escape. I was on the football team. My coach was not happy."

"But you were."

"Totally worth it. Although now I prefer quality over quantity."

Catherine brought their twined hands up to her lips and gave his a gentle kiss. "And may I say you are very good at what you do."

"Suddenly quantity seems like the best idea ever. There should be a turnoff soon. We can find a motel. Check in for a couple of hours."

"Tempting, but I'm too anxious to get where we're going."

He sighed, smiling. "I can't wait to see your face."

14

THE REST OF the five-hour trip flew by. They stopped for lunch at a place called Pat's Hubba Hubba, just off the interstate. She'd called in their order, and once they were back on the road, they ate their sinfully delicious hot dogs and chased them down with extrafizzy sodas.

When they arrived at their destination, the Dan'l Webster Inn & Spa in Sandwich, Massachusetts, Catherine was awestruck.

The colonial-style building was painted a stately deep red. With the lush grounds that surrounded it, it looked like something out of a movie. After stopping at reception, they were quickly escorted to a stunning luxury suite complete with a four-poster king bed, a sitting room, a spa tub set in its own half gazebo in an alcove next to the bedroom, and a view that looked out over the beautifully manicured garden and swimming pool.

Catherine should have tipped the bellman, but by the time she'd turned from the window, he was gone and Tony was putting his wallet back in his jeans pocket. The way he wore his jeans, low on the hips, made her stomach twist in the best possible way. "This is a wonderful surprise," she said, slowly making her way toward him, purposefully giving him time to plan his next move. "Better than what I had guessed."

"And what was that?"

"I'm not saying."

He laughed, making her grin. Of all his facial expressions, she liked this one the best. Then he sobered as he stared into her eyes, and she wondered if he could see how much this treat meant to her, and how she couldn't wait for him to lose the shirt and the jeans.

"I booked us both into the spa in about an hour and a half."

"Really? A couples massage?"

Tony walked over to the coffee table, where a bottle of champagne was chilling in an ice bucket. He picked the whole thing up and brought it over to the spa tub. Before he popped the cork, he turned on the water. "Thought about it, but no. I wanted you to pick whichever treatment you like best. And to have some alone time to chill."

He joined her, standing in front of the bed, where he pulled her into a kiss that melted her right down to her toes. His body pressed against her, all hard and taut, his blooming erection jutting against her hip.

"There's a lot we could do in an hour and a half," she whispered, before taking his earlobe between her teeth.

"Once I saw how your eyes lit up seeing the tub, I had the bellman cancel the bikes I reserved."

She leaned back. "Bikes?"

"It's a pretty town. Older than dust. There's a lot to see, and I know how much you like old buildings."

"So sweet," she said, kissing him quickly on the lips. "The most considerate man in the world." Kissing him again, she moved just enough so that she could unbutton his shirt from the top down.

"Old buildings are overrated, anyway," he said, seconds before he pulled her T-shirt over her head.

"We can use the bikes tomorrow morning," she said. "Maybe go find an interesting breakfast place, do some sightseeing before we have to leave.

"Great. I..." His voice trailed off as he came in for another round of kissing.

Somehow, they both ended up naked, and while the tub filled, he maneuvered her against the wall that separated the bedroom from the tub area. He pulled her arms high and held her wrists there with one hand while he did amazing things to her neck and collarbones. She'd have to dress carefully for a while to hide the marks he was leaving on her skin, which was more than fine by her.

Her moans were louder than they probably should have been, but she wasn't about to stop. When he let her go, Catherine lowered herself into the hot tub. Tony poured them champagne, then retrieved a small box of chocolates, and brought everything to within arm's reach. The whole time she checked him out with a thoroughness that would've made her squirm if their roles had been reversed. "You are by far," she said, "the best-looking naked man I've ever seen."

He might've grinned, but she didn't know for sure, since she couldn't drag her gaze away from his erection.

"Seen a lot, then, have you? Naked men?"

"My share. But none of them have made me feel like this."

"Like what?"

She blushed and burst into laughter.

His arm muscles bunched as he lowered himself into the water. "Come on, like what?" he said, as he handed her one of the flutes.

"Nope." She shook her head, then took a hurried sip of champagne.

Without missing a beat he leaned in and kissed the taste of the bubbly right off her tongue.

When he drew back, she chased his lips for a second, until she realized he was getting comfortable and settling into the tub directly across from her. Before she could stop herself, she stretched her foot between his legs to where his cock was bobbing delightfully. "What's your opinion on foot jobs?" she asked.

"I've never had one before," he said. "And while I think it's a great experiment to try, the timing could be better."

"You mean that I should wait until we're ready to get out?"

He nodded, his gaze sweeping down to her chest. "Not just out, but when we're ready to go to bed. Besides, I really like the view from here."

She glanced down at her naked breasts. "They are bouncing nicely, aren't they?"

"I'm so glad this isn't a bubble bath. We would have missed so much."

Her laughter made her jiggle and she saw the glint in his eyes. She grabbed her glass and sipped again. "This is exceptionally good champagne. In fact, this whole place is exceptional. Have you stayed here before?"

"No, I haven't. A friend recommended it if I ever came up this way."

"I love that this suite has the tub so close to the bed. Such a clever idea. And the amenities here are amazing. Did this champagne come with?"

"Champagne does come with, but this bottle was a special request."

God, she liked this man. More than she'd imagined

she could. It hadn't even been that long since the day they'd met, and yet he knew her in so many little ways. This was one of her top five champagnes, and she had no doubt that dinner would be as perfect.

He shifted, and she watched as he adjusted his body so the jets were more to his liking. Soaking in the tub like this did feel wonderful. Everywhere—but especially where his feet came to rest on the bench, bracketing her hips. That was all it took, evidently. Proximity. Any form of touch.

"How much of a pain in the ass would it be for me to have a spa tub on the roof?"

"A moderately big pain. It would add a lot of weight, and we're not even sure that you can get all your garden boxes and trees up there."

"And don't forget the pergola."

"I haven't. Or the windbreaks. But something like this? Maybe you could talk to Sal and see what it would take to put one in your new master bath."

"And risk him dropping dead on the spot?"

"You have a limited window of opportunity. And if you like, I can do some preliminary sketches, see what kind of plumbing issues we'd have. It's possible. That was good thinking, by the way, asking for an outside staircase that would require a key. Even if the rooftop community garden isn't viable—"

"Why wouldn't it be viable?"

He gave her an odd look. It reminded her of the day they'd first met. Damn, why couldn't she read him better by now? "The weight? City codes? Permits?"

"Ah, yes." Relaxing again, she waved at him to continue.

"Anyway, you'll most likely still be able to have a garden, but remember, if we can swing a tub, someone will need to take care of it. Unless you want to do all the maintenance yourself."

"I wouldn't mind that. I'm going to be up there, anyway, with the plants."

"In the dead of winter?"

"Winter is when the tub would be best."

"What the hell, then. Let's try to make it happen."

"If you weren't all the way over on the other side of the tub, I'd kiss you for that."

Tony shook his head. "You know I'd cross an entire bathtub for you. All you have to do is ask."

Catherine grabbed his ankles. He didn't even jump, but then he'd seen where her hands were headed. What he couldn't know was why she'd made her move. While trying to keep herself steady from the waist up, she spread her thighs very wide, then put his feet between them.

He nearly dropped his champagne. "Why, Ms. Fox, what an intriguing idea."

"One of us has to try out a foot job. Why not me?"

"I give you very high marks for creativity, but, um..."

"I realize it's not going to be as elegant as a hand job, but you have very nice feet, and they're very clean, so I don't think anything can go too wrong."

He put his glass behind him on the raised edge of the tub. "I think we should start with one foot."

"Hmm." She put his left foot back on the outside of her thigh. "Better?"

"Better. You'll let me know if I'm doing something you don't like, right?"

"So we're back to hot and cold?"

His grin got bigger as his pupils grew darker.

"Wait," she said, as she turned to the panel on the wall behind her back. She'd adjusted the jets already, and this time she went for the dimmer switch. Not a big change.

She still wanted to see his eyes, his chest. But there was something sexy about the shadows.

The flat of his forefoot landed gently on her labia. A shiver caught her unprepared, but it was a nice surprise. He wasn't even touching anything that sensitive, so it was the idea as much as the act that had her pulse racing.

She decided to let him explore unaided. At least for a while. There was very little chance that she would come from this game, but that was fine. She could wait until after dinner for the big fireworks.

Keeping the pad of his foot pressed against her, he rubbed her in small circles until his heel hit the tub seat. "If I move forward," she said, "you could reach lower, but you wouldn't have a stable base for your heel."

Moving his foot up, just as slowly, he didn't answer right away. "I think let's leave it for now."

The lowering of his voice told her what she wasn't able to see for herself. His erection had to be straining.

"Luckily for me," he said, "I know where the important bits are."

She giggled and smothered a hiccup. "Bits?"

He nodded. "Very important ones. Now hush. I'm concentrating."

Catherine hid her grin by drinking more, but a moment later, he stopped moving.

"Scratch that hush," he said. "Sounds are good. All the sounds. Anything you'd like to share."

"Okay, then," she said, although she hadn't planned on keeping silent. As he carefully slipped his very dexterous toes between her lips, she didn't hold back at all. It was a crazy, beautiful way to feel him. It made her like him even more, which hadn't seemed possible.

Her eyes closed as his big toe found her clit. He made his slow, somewhat jerky circles count, never coming close to making her uncomfortable. She felt as if the bubbles of the Dom Perignon had become the bubbles from the jets, filling her with light and magic as he took his sweet time giving her pleasure.

It occurred to her in the middle of yet another shiver that she'd been wrong. Or at least hadn't been completely honest with herself. She didn't just like Tony. He wasn't perfect, which was good, because perfection would lose its luster quickly. He was very human. And it wasn't just his looks she was crazy about, although they certainly helped. It was far more than that.

He treated her the way she'd always wanted to be treated. He made love to her the way she'd fantasized about for most of her adult life. He touched her heart, her mind, her sense of humor. Clearly, he admired her for who she was, just as she admired him. She wouldn't change one thing about the man.

Except to make him stay with her for keeps.

God, she was in so much trouble.

TONY SIPPED HIS pinot noir as he watched Catherine talk to one of the staff at Diamond Hill Vineyards. It was just past 2:00 p.m., and they'd had an amazing day already. But that wasn't what he was picturing when he heard Catherine laugh.

Last night had been a revelation. After an excellent meal, they'd gone back to their room, where they stripped each other bare before they were two feet from the door. He'd carried her to the big four-poster bed, and then he'd taken his sweet time making her lose her mind.

She'd done the same to him, effortlessly. Listening to her moan as he'd tasted her sea salt and Catherine juices, he'd almost come before she'd even touched him. And watching her come? He forgot to breathe until he had to take a life-saving gasp. Grateful to be alive, he'd followed up by entering her in time to feel the tail end of her aftershocks.

The scratches on his back were worth the momentary pain. Trophies he wanted to feel for as long as possible. Then he figured he'd repeat the winning formula, perhaps with a few surprises thrown in, so she'd mark him again.

God, she'd been something else. He'd seen stars when he'd finally come. They'd celebrated, once they'd gotten their breath back, by having another dip in the spa, finished the rest of the champagne and chocolates, and he'd actually made her come right there surrounded by bubbling water.

By the time they were dried off, they'd collapsed in bed, and fallen asleep instantly. This morning, he'd woken to her clutching him, leg over his, arm over his chest, head tucked onto the dip of his shoulder. It felt great.

A little too great, if he thought about it, but instead, he'd roused her in his own special way, then they'd showered together, gotten their bicycles and found a nice little café that made excellent French toast and coffee.

They'd even taken a walk by the bay. It had been a great stroll. Nothing better than draping his arm around her shoulders while she slipped her left hand into his back pocket.

She'd found the winery on her cell phone, and they'd decided to stop at the gorgeous old place in Cumberland, Rhode Island. She'd discovered how much she liked their pinot noir, and before he knew it, he was putting a case in the trunk.

Then it was time to hit the interstate again, heading toward one more stop before they returned to Little Italy. Another surprise. One he thought she'd like a lot.

In fact, when he turned into the big ironworks in New Haven, Connecticut, Catherine gripped his arm so hard he thought she might leave bruises. "Iron Works?" she said, her voice starting the question in one pitch, but ending somewhere completely different. "This is the metalworker. Your friend who's going to help with my house."

Tony nodded. "Dave has a few drawings he wants to show you before he comes down to do the measurements."

Her mouth opened but nothing came out for a minute. "This has been the best surprise trip ever."

"I don't know about ever, but I think it worked out pretty well."

"You put so much thought into it. I don't know that anyone's ever tailored a getaway to my tastes so perfectly."

"It's my pleasure," he said, meaning every word.

"Are we going to actually order things today, or is this just a fact-finding mission?"

"Well, they're not technically open today, although a few of his guys are working. But I suppose if you wanted to order some things, it would be fine. I told him about your place and sent him pictures. I know he's drawn up a few things so you'll see how we can best match your vision."

They parked near the entrance to the large building, and Catherine jumped out as soon as Tony turned off the engine.

She was next to him quickly, grabbing his hand with both of hers, but she let go just as fast. "Wait. Am I supposed to be a client and nothing more?"

"You be whatever feels comfortable," he said, just as his friend, Dave, met them at the door. He was a big man, muscled from his work at the forge. As he shook Catherine's hand, Tony said, "Dave's taken over this business from his father."

"And grandfather," Dave said, giving Tony a slap on the back. Thankfully, Tony was used to the greeting. First time he'd been at the receiving end, he'd nearly fallen flat on his face.

"I like your house," Dave said, turning to Catherine. "My office is upstairs. I'll show you some of my drawings. You tell me what you like, what you're not crazy about. Then I'll take you through the gallery, so you can get a good look at some alternatives, and we'll see what comes of that. You have a camera with you?"

"My cell phone."

"It'll do fine," he said, leading them inside.

The space was well ventilated, but it still smelled like fire and something very primal. Tony knew Dave and his crew worked in steel, iron, aluminum and probably other mediums, and it was that primal scent that made him take a deep breath. The clang of a hammer on metal resonated through the whole structure.

She was all eyes and wonder as they climbed up to the office. In minutes they had settled in comfortable chairs around a table, coffee mugs in front of them, with Tony able to watch Catherine's expressive face.

"Look," she said, beckoning him to lean in to see the drawings for the staircase. Dave had really listened about the art deco style she liked, and what he was showing her blew them both away.

"They're gorgeous. I want them all, but I think I like the idea of the wavy design with the walnut handrail best. God, the twisted balusters are stunning. Although, what you did with this other one with the painted mural..." She ended with a sigh.

"I'll make copies of the drawings, all of them, then when you go back home, you can decide."

Tony could tell she wanted to be teleported home right that moment. Although he could easily see any of the designs would work well. They went on to look at Dave's designs for the fireplaces, the front stoop and a private exterior spiral staircase up to the roof.

It took them almost two hours to finish with Dave and to load the standing lamp, the wall art and bookends Catherine had purchased into the trunk of the car. Dave seemed a little surprised by her hug at the end. Tony was, too. She wasn't a hugger. But the man had brought the goods.

She slid into the passenger seat, and halfway down the driveway, she made Tony stop the car so she could kiss him. It was all he could do not to tell himself to turn around and go back to the hotel, the hell with work.

God, he liked this woman. Too much. Far too much.

15

TONY SLOWED HIS STEPS as he realized just how much he'd rushed since getting off the subway near Catherine's. No need to bring more attention to himself than he was already getting from the neighborhood gossips. It was just that he'd seen her only once in the week since they'd gotten back from their getaway, and while they'd finished replacing the tiles on both fireplaces, they'd both been too exhausted to make love, and, well, he'd fallen asleep. She'd shaken him awake at about one in the morning and sent him home.

Today was different. It was Saturday, and while they were going to work on the sconces, he planned on doing his best work once they got into bed. He'd missed her.

Just as he arrived at her front stoop, his cell phone rang with her tone. Confused, he hit the button and said, "Catherine?"

"Am I interrupting?" Her voice was like auditory sex, low with just the perfect amount of huskiness.

"Not at all."

"I was wondering what you were doing for the next couple of hours."

The next... *Ah*. He recognized where this conversation was going. "Working on your house?"

"Can I get you to change your mind?

"Depends on the alternative."

She laughed. "Look up."

He saw her, standing at her second-floor window. Her grin lit him up inside.

"I'd like to take you somewhere."

"You realize I'm in my work clothes."

"Doesn't matter. You still look hot as hell."

Tony smiled. "Don't know what to say to that."

"Oh, that's fine. I'm perfectly okay with you just being arm candy."

He let out a laugh, catching the attention of two little girls playing hopscotch on the sidewalk.

"Stay right there. I'll be down in a second."

It was more than a second, but he didn't mind. She looked happy and gorgeous in worn, tight-fitting jeans and a dusky pink blouse, and the only part he didn't like was that he couldn't kiss her. The whole block of busybodies would probably implode.

"Let's go," she said, almost taking his hand before she caught herself, and all he got was an apologetic smile instead of that kiss he wanted.

"Where to?"

"Not far."

"You have me intrigued, Ms. Fox."

"Good. That's right where I want you."

"Oh, I have someplace completely different in mind," he said, lowering his voice and giving her a heated look that made her blush.

"Stop it. There are kids playing around here."

Tony smiled and nodded at one of the neighborhood

boys coming toward them on a skateboard. "Hey, Mickey, you get that for your birthday?"

"Yeah, yesterday."

"Nice, but watch you don't get too close to the street, huh?"

"I won't, Mr. Paladino," he said, clearly not interested in the advice.

Catherine gave Tony a particularly sweet smile.

"What?"

"Nothing. It's just—it's nice that you look out for the kids, that's all." she said, shrugging. "You know everyone, don't you?"

"I'm sure I've overlooked a few people." He took in her flushed cheeks and shining blue eyes and wondered if he'd ever felt this damned happy just walking down the street. Not a clue as to where he was headed. And not giving a shit, either. "I wonder what would happen if I took your hand and held it all the way to..." He frowned. "Wherever the hell we're going."

"Well, I'm guessing I'd get a lot of street cred. You, however, would get a call from your mom in, oh, about five minutes."

"Five?" Tony laughed. "You underestimate the grapevine."

As if to illustrate the point, three ladies, older women Catherine didn't recognize, moved right in front of Tony before they made it to the corner. "Tony," the taller one said. "You're working today?"

"Yes, Mrs. La Bianca. This is my friend and client, Ms. Fox."

The woman barely nodded. "I hear you moved next to Ida Masucci."

"You did?" Catherine gave her an innocent smile.

"I hear things," she said. "This is a very close neighborhood. We've all known each other since we were born. Our families have lived here for generations."

Before Catherine could respond, the woman with the white hair said, "I understand your Angie is still single. Working outside the neighborhood. Such a shame. You were such a happy couple. But then, she's like us, a part of the community."

Tony wasn't going to let this continue. He touched Catherine behind her elbow. "I don't want to be late," he said, stepping around the rude *pettegole*.

Catherine didn't say a word, and it took him the rest of the block to calm down. They got to Delancey and Orchard, managing to keep a polite distance from each other. But all he wanted to do was take her away again. As far as necessary.

At this point he wasn't worried about their business relationship. He was handling that part just fine. Not one client or job had suffered while he took a little time to have a life. It was subjecting Catherine to her nosy, judgmental neighbors that stopped him. He couldn't think of a quicker way to send her packing, and he couldn't bear the thought.

She came to a stop in front of the bookstore on the corner. "It's okay, Tony. I know your ex was part of the community. The comments make sense. I don't mind."

"You have every right to mind like hell. That was intolerably rude."

"You handled it very well, and now we're here, and I want us to have a good time. You think we can?"

He took a deep breath and nodded. "Of course we can."

"Good. I hope you're not disappointed. I realize you've probably been here dozens of times."

"The bookstore?"

"No, the museum."

He looked again at what was directly in front of him. "Right. The Tenement Museum."

"Do you mind going again?"

"To be honest, I haven't technically been here before."

She lifted an eyebrow. "Technically?"

"Paladino & Sons are sustaining donors. Have been since the first year, before it even opened. But, I don't know. It's like that old saying, 'The cobbler's kids have no shoes'? No, wait, I didn't mean that one."

"It's all right. I get your point. So, interested in seeing it now?"

"With you? Sure."

Her hand moved to take his, but she switched it up at the last minute, as if she had to cover a cough. Jesus. The charade was getting old. They entered the museum shop and joined a group of tourists listening to a spiel about the rules. Tony had to keep his thoughts to himself when the rule about no touching came up. They meant the rooms, the displays, of course, but all he could do was look at how beautiful Catherine was with her hair pinned up. He loved it the other way, too, but this showed off her long graceful neck, and damn, he wanted a taste. Right now. Screw everybody.

"Tony?"

He met her gaze. "Yeah?"

"We're starting now."

"Right. Sorry. Got caught up thinking."

"Are you sure you want to do this? It won't hurt my feelings if you don't."

"I really do."

"Then come on. I don't want to miss anything."

They caught up to the group a minute later. There were fifteen people, most of whom were German tourists. As the museum employee told them about the time frames of the great immigration movements from Europe during the late-eighteenth and early-nineteenth centuries, Tony watched Catherine. She was captivated. Unguardedly joyful. Every part of her was present in the way that few people in his life were. Most people listened with half an ear, waiting for their phones to ring. Not Catherine. She was all or nothing. It felt as if the only time he could focus his thoughts on a single topic was when he was with her.

Although after each visit, the jolt back to his regular life was becoming more difficult.

It had been risky to engage in an affair with a client. Let alone when he'd just taken over the business. He'd felt guilty about it in the beginning, but not anymore.

He had to admit, he was dreading the day when she realized she would never belong to the private members club that was his neighborhood. If he could, he'd protect her from that forever. But she wasn't one of the new crop of tenants who didn't give a crap about Little Italy. To most of them, the idea of the old neighborhood had overstayed its welcome years ago. Just her bad luck that she'd bought one of the very last single-family homes in the whole area, probably the most coveted house in the Lower East Side.

It had always bothered him that he and Catherine couldn't be openly together, but now it was becoming a steady ache. If it was just him who'd be affected, Tony would have told them all to go to hell. Catherine, though... He cared a lot that she'd be considered even more of a pariah than she already was.

The tour reached the second floor, the one-time apartment of the Baldizzi family. He didn't recognize the name, but he knew if he went back to the archives his family had collected—copies of census forms, birth and death records, anything they could gather from the time period—the Baldizzis would be there. It was this world his great-great-grandparents had occupied, in a building just like this one.

His brilliant great-great-grandfather, who'd seen the future, had invested every penny he and his brothers had earned into real estate. Tony had mentioned something about it to Catherine when she'd asked about his parents' home. But he'd been careful. No one who wasn't family could know about the trust. About the buildings the Paladinos owned in and around Little Italy.

It was just another barrier between the two of them.

The tour was on the move again, filing from the preserved tiny kitchen into a room that had been modified as New York had passed laws to make these horrible squats more bearable.

He turned to Catherine to tell her about what it had been like before indoor plumbing, but the educator got to her first.

"Hey, Catherine," the guy said.

"Hey, Vito," she said. "Great tour, as always. You do such a wonderful job." She looked to Tony and told the museum employee, "By the way, this is my friend Tony Paladino. He's lived here all his life but he's never been to the museum before."

The guy, who looked to be a few years younger than Tony, held out his hand. "Nice to meet you in person. We all appreciate what the Paladino family has done for the museum. Catherine's a regular here. I hope you'll become one, as well."

Tony just nodded, feeling a little uncomfortable to be singled out. Good thing he'd already mentioned his family's involvement to her, not that it was a big deal...

"Well, we both love the history of the Lower East Side," Catherine said. "And I learn something new every time I'm here."

"You could be giving the tours already. Hey, you know, you should really think about volunteering. Anyway, just wanted to say hello. I need to..." He pointed his thumb behind him, at the group.

"See you soon," she said.

"How many times have you been here?" Tony asked.

She turned to him, jumping a little when she realized how close he was standing.

He hadn't realized he'd moved, much less that he was close enough to her to feel her breath on his chin. Her lips were parted, her eyes alive with excitement, so he stayed right where he was and took her hand in his. "There's nothing decorative that you could use for your home in here, is there? I mean, the walls are covered in burlap. The floors are new, the window coverings, too, I think."

"It's not about finding things for my place. I truly do love this area, and I want to know as much as I can about it. Besides, they have several tours, not just this one. The things they've unearthed from so many decades ago are amazing. It's one of my favorite places."

"Huh. I learn something new about you every time I see you."

"Every time?"

"Just about." It would be so easy to lean down and kiss her. The temptation was so great he wasn't sure he would be able to resist.

"We don't have to stay, if you don't want to. It's a long tour."

"No, I want you to enjoy yourself. I'm having a good time."

She looked down at their joined hands. "Is this a wise idea?"

"Everyone here is a tourist."

"Not everyone." She glanced over her shoulder at Vito. "He lives off Bowery. Knows a lot of people. Part of the reason I come here so often is because of the volunteers. Not all of them live in the neighborhood, but, like Vito—" she lowered her voice, even though she'd been whispering "—like Vito, they've been very welcoming."

"You still haven't met your next-door neighbors, have you?"

"Not officially. Although I have run into them a few times."

Tony let go of her hand. It was shitty that no one had dropped by to officially welcome her. Naturally, he'd known the two old ladies wouldn't say boo to her, but he'd figured Deanna, Mrs. Masucci's daughter, might stop by. Or maybe Isabel from across the street, even if only to indulge her own curiosity. He hated that Catherine would end up so disillusioned.

Maybe he should have warned her that first day they'd met. Although if anyone had a chance to win over some of these archaic, narrow-minded folks, it was Catherine.

"We should go," she said, taking hold of his shirtsleeve and pulling him back from the latest exhibit.

"Why?"

"You don't look like you're having a good time."

"I am," he said, his voice loudly interrupting the lecture. He winced and held up an apologetic hand, then let Catherine lead the way out.

On the stairs, out of hearing range, he stopped her. "I'm sorry. I didn't mean to spoil this adventure. I was enjoying it."

"Until Vito came by."

Tony could instantly feel his face flush. "It had nothing to do with him. I'm embarrassed I haven't been here before. We can continue with the tour. I promise to be good."

"Oh, I know exactly how good you are. Let's go. I really do want to finish the sconces."

"Is that all?"

She grinned. "As if you haven't been thinking about it since you fell asleep on me the other night."

He checked the stairwell, and then pulled her close into a kiss. He didn't linger, though. "You're right. I haven't stopped thinking about you for days."

"Believe me, it's mutual. And while I'm feeling brave, I wanted to ask you if you'd consider being my date at the World Health Organization banquet. It's not until next month, but—"

"Yeah, sure." He felt an odd kind of relief, as though he'd subconsciously been waiting for her to ask. "Count on it."

"It's black tie."

"No worries. So, home or tour?"

"Home," she decided. "I want to kiss you properly."

He took her hand and pulled her down the stairs, not really bothering to keep too much distance between them. The rumors would come, regardless, although when he got closer to her block, he'd be more careful.

He resented it. Again. Even though it had all been his idea. What he wanted was to just say fuck it, and kiss her right in the middle of Mulberry Street teeming with pedestrians. But thinking it through, he knew there would be consequences, and he'd do anything he could to make sure this amazing woman didn't get her heart broken.

16

THE SCENT OF citrus came first, seconds before the light behind his closed eyelids stirred him from a very sound sleep. That Catherine's head rested on his chest and her arm lay across him a few inches down made him hum.

Waking to a naked Catherine was a damn fine thing.

"I like this," she said, and he felt her warm breath on his skin. "You're a very comfortable body pillow."

"Glad I could oblige," he said, his voice sleep-filled and rough. "I don't want to move. Maybe not ever again. Would that be okay?"

"Absolutely. We have everything we need, right? Wine. Cookies. Yep, that's it."

"Sounds great," he murmured. "Although if we could turn off the light, that would be better."

She rubbed her foot up his calf and pressed her body closer. "Uh, I don't think that's possible."

"No?"

"I haven't been able to control the sun in ages," she said. "And I don't have blackout curtains."

Tony stilled. Then opened his eyes. "Shit."

"Um, I can always buy some."

"No. It's not…" He turned his head just far enough to

see the clock on her nightstand. It was a quarter to eight. In the fucking *morning*.

"I know what. Let's have a quickie, then shower, then go get breakfast at Katz's." She kissed him on the shoulder. "I want eggs and bagels."

"I can't."

"Oh?" Catherine raised her head to look at him. "Something's wrong."

"We fell asleep."

"Well, yes. We had very vigorous sex and then we both conked out."

The bells from the church on Mott rang out, and he knew he had to get up now. Right now. He kissed her forehead. "I've got to get going."

"But it's Sunday."

"Exactly. It's my turn to take my folks and Nonna to Mass. I'll barely make it in time. I'm going to take a quick shower, if that's okay. Or, no. Wait." He hated to do it, but he had to untangle himself from Catherine. "I'll call Luca. Maybe he can take them." At least Tony's jeans weren't far, just on the floor next to the bed.

Damn it. This was not good. As he hit the speed dial button for Luca, he realized he had no choice but to wear the clothes he'd worn yesterday. No way that would escape the eyes that always seemed to be on him these days.

"No answer?"

He shook his head. "Dom's not even around today, or I'd have him go. I can't not take them. And later I have to…" He shook his head. "Nothing. Just family stuff."

Catherine sat up, pulling the sheet over her breasts as she leaned against the headboard. "I'm assuming the unfortunate part is you having to leave my house in broad daylight?"

"Everyone's going to church, and a lot of them walk. It's not very far from here."

"I'm sorry. I know you've wanted to avoid this. I imagine it won't do your business any good if this gets around."

He stood, slid on his jeans. "I'm not worried about me. Or the company. It's you I'm concerned about."

"Me? I don't care. Let them talk. They'll get bored with me eventually."

He sighed. "You don't understand."

She frowned, looking confused, maybe a little hurt, and it bothered him that he couldn't stay. But he had to be on time; his mother had a thing about being late for Mass. But there was no way he was leaving Catherine like this. He sat back down on the bed, leaned over and kissed her. "It's fine. Honest."

"You know, if people are busy getting their kids and themselves ready for church, I bet they don't even notice you," she said.

"You're probably right." So many people and all those windows? Not a chance in hell. But he knew she was trying to make him feel better, and he smiled. Her expression told him he'd missed the mark. "Damn it, I hate abandoning you like this."

She opened her mouth, but she must have changed her mind because she closed it again, and gave him a smile that didn't reach her eyes.

"I'm sorry," he whispered, brushing the back of his fingers across her pale cheek.

"It's okay. Go. In fact, how about I call you a cab? Less chance that you'll be spotted."

"Good thinking. Thanks." He kissed her one more time, then grabbed his shirt off the chair against the wall, his socks and shoes, and hurried into the bathroom.

It wasn't just getting his family to Mass. He'd drop them off, go home to shower and change, then go back to the church to take his father home. There'd be another run to the church later. His mother and Nonna helped in the kitchens in the afternoon, with their women's group, making food for the Bowery homeless shelter and meals for the housebound members of the congregation. It was that gathering of women he was most concerned about.

If someone saw him leave Catherine's, which he knew was highly likely, that was where they'd talk. But would they talk about him when his mother was right there?

What was he thinking? Of course they would. They lived for this kind of bullshit. They'd be filled with false sympathy. Poor Theresa, whose oldest boy couldn't keep away from the *medigan* and was making a fool of himself in front of everyone. And with a client, no less. Hell, even if no one brought it up at the women's group, word would spread. His father would be disappointed. And so soon after Tony had taken over for him.

Oddly, none of that mattered to him half as much as the blowback Catherine would suffer. If his mom had to put up with the gossip, that was her problem. She wasn't shy about speaking her mind; she could tell them to mind their own damn business. As for his father, Tony was handling the office just fine.

But Catherine had no idea that this kind of talk could be what drove her out of the community she wanted so much to embrace her. He'd seen it happen to people who weren't nearly as invested in belonging.

He finished brushing his teeth with the only thing he kept at Catherine's, ran his fingers through his hair, kissed her, then headed downstairs. Leaving Catherine this way was shitty. He'd make it up to her, though. Somehow.

He breathed a sigh of relief when he saw the cab waiting at the curb. But he couldn't stop thinking about how awkward it had been between them.

As CATHERINE WALKED down Grand, she couldn't stop thinking about what had happened with Tony. He'd finally spent the night at her house, something she'd wanted for a while. But his brushing her aside with the quick and generic excuse of having to do "family stuff" made her uncomfortable. She'd already met them—what was he trying to hide?

But the real heart of her problem was his certainty that something terrible was going to happen because he'd spent the night.

There were a couple reasons she could think of that might explain his irrational fear. It was possible that rumors had caused him a lot of grief before. Something to do with his ex-wife, perhaps? It certainly seemed as though his precious community thought their divorce was a horrible mistake.

That, or else he believed that some of the neighbors were so vicious that he'd lose customers over sleeping with a client. That seemed extreme, especially given how highly regarded Paladino & Sons were in the community. Still, she supposed it could be what was worrying him.

She wasn't going to confront Tony. Being the temporary woman in his life didn't give her that right.

For another long block, she tried to make peace with the fact that, by tacit agreement, being the temp was what she'd signed up for. If she didn't like it, she could call a halt to the whole thing.

The thought left her feeling incredibly sad.

By the time she reached Broadway, it occurred to her that there was nothing to be gained by sitting back and letting things happen to her. She'd never been that person. If she wanted something, she needed to take action.

Perhaps she'd been remiss in not introducing herself to her neighbors, assuring them that the noise coming from her house was temporary and she wouldn't be ruining the neighborhood. It seemed likely that no welcoming committee was forthcoming, and she couldn't blame anyone for that. The longer the situation went on, the more difficult it would be for even those with the best intentions.

The ball was in her court.

Hailing a taxi, she asked the driver to take her to the Lady M Boutique in Bryant Park, where she bought two mille crêpes signature cakes. Half an hour later, she had one beautifully boxed cake in hand as she knocked on the door of her neighbor Mrs. Masucci.

Someone else opened the door. A woman in her early thirties, with a cute bob haircut and a pretty sundress. Catherine recognized her. They hadn't spoken but they'd nodded to each other, and the woman she assumed was Mrs. Masucci's daughter had smiled.

"Hi, I'm Catherine Fox. Your next-door neighbor."

"Yes, I've seen you." She stepped back, opening the door wide. "It's nice to meet you. I'm Deanna Alberti. Please, come in."

The house was much more modern than Catherine had expected. It had an open floor plan, a beautiful wooden staircase, and the kitchen was large with two ovens, a chef's range and a double fridge.

Catherine held up the cake box. "I'm sorry it's not homemade, but I'm afraid my kitchen is still under construction."

"That's very kind," Deanna said. "Lady M? I've only been there once, but I'll never forget that éclair."

"I love it too much," Catherine said, shaking her head.

"You have no idea how many miles I've clocked on the stationary bike because of that evil place. I think I've pedaled across the Atlantic already."

"I hear you. I was thinking of having a coffee. Can I tempt you to join me?"

"I'd love that, thank you."

After leading her to the kitchen, Deanna went about fixing a pot of dark roast. Catherine had thought a lot about what to say on her way over, so after taking a seat at the big marble island, she dived right in. "I'm so sorry I haven't introduced myself before now. My work schedule has been heavy, and then there's been all the construction. I'm sure you all hate me for the noise. But I promise the loud part will be over soon."

"I know what it's like to remodel. This whole floor was redone two years ago, just before my family and I moved back from upstate. We live on the ground floor, and my mother's suite is on the top floor. We share this space, and try to cook and eat as a family, although we're all so busy, dinner is hit and miss."

"It must be wonderful, though, when you manage it."

"Your family isn't here?"

"No. They're in Europe. I don't get to see them that often."

"That must be lonely."

"I have work friends, which is nice. I figure it'll take me some time to find my place here. Although it'll be a lot easier once the house is finished."

Deanna seemed puzzled, but she turned away to get two mugs down from the cupboard. "I didn't realize you were staying," she said.

"Yes, everyone assumes I'm going to flip the house."

"Well, there's a lot of that happening around here now.

Everything's changed so much since I was a kid. Little Italy had a real presence then, not just a few blocks."

Catherine nodded. "I've seen pictures and heard a lot about the neighborhood from the fifties through the eighties. Did you know the Calabrese family that used to live next door?"

"All my life. But after their mother died, the kids all wanted to go in different directions."

"That's how I came to the house, actually. You knew Belaflore, then?"

"Ah, the grandmother." Deanna shook her head. "I know of her, but she had already gone before I was born. I think she left the country to work for a diplomat or ambassador. Something along those lines."

"My family. She was my nanny. The person I was closest to in the world. She used to tell me stories about when she lived here. When the house came up for sale, I had to have it. It felt as if I already knew the neighborhood. Probably because I associated it with Belaflore," Catherine said, feeling nostalgic. "We moved around so much I never really had a place that I could call home, and this felt right."

"Oh, God. I feel terrible that I didn't go over and introduce myself. We thought you'd sell it and be out of here."

"It's fine, really," Catherine said, although she couldn't deny the relief she felt over realizing she hadn't been snubbed.

"Well, I'm glad you came over." Deanna handed her a mug of coffee. "Cream? Sugar?"

"Sugar, thanks."

After Deanna sat down, she opened the cake box. Her smile lit up her face. "This is their famous cake, right? The mille crêpes? It's like eighty dollars or something." She brought out a cake plate, but as she opened a drawer of utensils, she stopped still. "That was tactless of me. I'm sorry. It's just that I have two kids—I'm sure you've heard their big mouths—so I never dreamed I'd be getting a taste of this. Now, Twinkies I'm familiar with."

Catherine laughed. "No problem." She liked the woman even more.

"Would you like a slice?"

Catherine shook her head. "It's all yours. Go for it."

Deanna took her seat once more. Catherine was so pleased about how things were going she wanted to kick herself for not doing this sooner. "I know it sounds silly, but my view of the house, of the whole neighborhood, was very romantic. Belaflore should have been a writer. She told the most wonderful stories. It wasn't until I started looking into the history of the place that I discovered some of what she'd described. Now I can't get enough of the beautiful artifacts from the twenties and thirties. Fortunately, my contractor is helping me tremendously. He's very well acquainted with restoration."

Deanna smiled. "Tony Paladino." It wasn't a question. She'd obviously seen Tony coming and going. Thankfully, there wasn't anything mean or judgmental in her expression. "You're lucky."

Catherine braced herself. *Please, don't let this conversation turn personal.*

"They're the most reliable contractors in the Lower East Side. They did all of the work in this house."

"Ah." Catherine relaxed and glanced around. "Very nice."

"All three brothers are really good guys, and they were weaned on construction. I've known them forever. I was a year behind Tony in school," Deanna said with a spark of mischief in her eye. "He was pretty notorious back in the day."

Catherine tried not to show any reaction to the woman's teasing. "Oh?"

"Yeah. Of course you have to know he was the best-looking guy in his class. It wasn't fair, really. All three brothers were hit hard with the handsome stick. But Tony. He was a jock—the quarterback, naturally. Every girl wanted him."

"Did he end up with the head cheerleader?"

"No. He didn't really have a girlfriend until middle of junior year. That's when he hooked up with Angie. They were on and off for a while, but eventually they got married. As I'm sure you know, it didn't work out. I don't think I ever heard the real reason why. Just rumors."

"Those do run pretty thick down those streets."

Deanna rolled her eyes as she chuckled. "It's the most important currency in town, especially for my mother's generation. They were all stay-at-home moms or they worked in the family shops. I think it's still a bone of contention that many of their daughters want to have their own jobs and be independent."

"I can imagine."

"It gives them something to talk about after church."

Catherine sipped her coffee, hoping she and Tony weren't today's topic of conversation. Then she thought about his mother, and wondered if that attitude toward working mothers had been instrumental in Tony's breakup with Angie.

"I wanted to mention that I'm installing a rooftop garden," Catherine said. "Six sizable raised beds for vegetables, a small greenhouse for winter, some trees and flowers. I'm having a separate entryway built so that you and your family, and other neighbors, can plant and harvest whatever you grow."

"Seriously?" Deanna seemed genuinely excited. "That's very generous."

"I caught the bug at work. We have community gardens that are lovely. It's such a great way to meet people. Unfortunately, there's going to be a crane involved, but not for long. Just know I'm not doing it to punish anyone. It should only take a day for everything to be lifted up."

"I think that's a wonder—"

Behind Catherine, the front door opened. One look at Deanna's face told her that Mrs. Masucci had come home.

"Mama," she said. "Mrs. Soriano. I've made fresh coffee. And look, we have a guest. She brought this amazing cake for us. Isn't that nice?"

Catherine stood and faced her two neighbors. Yes, these were the two women she'd bumped into before. "Hello. I'm Catherine Fox. I live in the old Calabrese house." She held out her hand to Mrs. Masucci first. Instead of a ready hand, she was given a look that was equal parts surprise and shock. Then the hand came out and it was like shaking a cold, wet noodle. But Catherine didn't give up.

She held her hand out to Mrs. Soriano. "And of course, we've met. I was going to come properly introduce myself later today. I'm so sorry it's taken me this long."

The return handshake was just as unenthusiastic. Both women were clearly not pleased that she'd come by.

"Catherine's installing a rooftop garden next door," Deanna said, trying hard to sound upbeat. "And she's invited us to plant whatever vegetables we'd like. She's even putting in a separate access so we can come and go."

Mrs. Masucci nodded, as neutral a comment as was possible. Then she leaned slightly to her right, and said in Italian, "It's from a bakery. What kind of person doesn't do her own baking?"

"She doesn't know better," Mrs. Soriano replied, also in Italian.

"Mom," Deanna said, her tone sharp. Embarrassed. "It's extremely generous of Catherine to offer her garden space. You're always saying it's a shame we have no real garden."

"I grow tomatoes in the pots," her mother said, this time in English. "They do well."

"Yes," Deanna said. "But we'll be able to grow lettuce, peppers. Whatever we like."

Her mother, who must have been in her late sixties, stood with a straight back and an uncompromising gaze. There was no attempt to make Catherine feel welcome. In fact, it was just the opposite. The older woman shifted her handbag to her other arm. "So, you'll be putting the house up for sale when you finish?"

"Actually, no." Catherine stood up straighter herself, although she didn't want to make Deanna feel uncomfortable. "I'm planning on staying."

Her Italian whisper carrying well into the kitchen, Mrs. Soriano muttered, "Not if we can help it."

Catherine turned and smiled at Deanna, who was staring daggers at the older ladies. "Thank you for the coffee. I really must be going." She turned to the two women and in perfect Italian said, "And thank you for your kind welcome to the area. This visit has been very enlightening."

Then she walked out of the house without looking back, went straight into her own kitchen, where she'd left the cake for Mrs. Soriano, and dropped the entire thing into the garbage.

17

FINALLY, GEORGE HAD come through with the glass blocks for the master shower to match the originals that Tony and Catherine had discovered were in one of the earliest designs. They'd been delivered on Tuesday, and Tony was able to book the rooftop garden designer to come on Wednesday evening. But none of that mattered now. Tony had been very anxious to see Catherine. Since he'd left her on Sunday, they'd talked on the phone, but she'd worked late two nights. He'd apologized again and told her he'd put together some clothes to leave at her house... just in case. He'd thought they'd worked things out.

Now that the plumbing and hardware were complete in the master bathroom, he and Catherine were installing the semiopaque glass. The job wasn't difficult. Aside from the material, it was simple masonry, which he'd been doing since he was a kid. He'd gotten to her place on time, having cleared his schedule to meet her just after she'd arrived home from work. She'd even put on music that was from this decade, which was a nice change from classical.

And yet...

Something was wrong. He'd noticed it immediately.

Catherine had kissed him hello, but it had been quick, perfunctory. Which in itself wasn't alarming. But that had been only the tip of the iceberg. She didn't seem excited about the wall and she should have been. Had been when they'd discussed it. And she was able to participate because the project was just her speed. She'd come to like feeling as if she was part of the restoration process. It was her chance to make the shower her own, show off how much she'd learned. She loved that stuff. But he hesitated to say anything. Maybe she was just having one of those days. Maybe something had happened at work. Maybe a lot of things.

If she hadn't kept avoiding his gaze, he wouldn't have brought it up, but he couldn't not, "Catherine?"

"Yes?" she said, too quickly. Too brightly.

"Is everything okay?"

"Of course," she said, giving him a token smile before she focused on the next block. "Everything's fine."

He set down his trowel, covered the mortar and put his hands on her shoulders. She jumped at the contact. "I might be able to help if you tell me what's going on."

She took a deep breath and finally looked at him. "I'm sorry to drop a bomb so late in the game, but I've been doing a lot of thinking. I've decided to scale back my plans for the garden."

He could feel her tense under his hands, so he let her go, but stayed close. "What do you mean, scale back?"

"A community garden is a lot of work. I think I'm going to just do a couple of raised beds, enough for my own use. And, you know, it was kind of ridiculous to think about a whirlpool up there. I'll probably just go with the greenhouse instead, and four trees should be plenty. Oh, and I'll need to cancel the outdoor staircase."

The way she talked was utterly unlike her. It was as if her inner light had dimmed. He hated it. "Is this about the cost?"

"No. I told you, that's not the problem."

"You could hire people to maintain the garden and the tub. All of it. Tailor it to your needs."

"Thanks. I know. I didn't want it to be like that, though. And with the unpredictable winters here—I don't know. It just feels like too much."

"I'm confused. Did something happen? Did I do or say—?"

"No. I've just changed my mind, that's all."

She went over to her newly installed tempered glass sink and washed her hands. No grinning, no playing with the hardware. It had taken her forever to decide on the precise color of that damn sink, and it was far too new to have become part of the wallpaper.

"Seriously. It's not about you at all," she said. "In fact, I finally understand what you meant about the neighborhood. Don't worry about it, though. Everything's fine. I mean, now is the time to change my mind, right? I'll pay for the staircase if he's already built it. Anyway, I didn't give up on my jetted bathtub…" She sighed as she dried her hands, then turned back to him. Her smile was sweet and sad. And when she pulled him down for a kiss, he could almost taste her melancholy.

It was bewildering. This wasn't his Catherine. "When you said you understand what I meant…did one of your neighbors come by and act like a jerk?"

"No. But I did go next door."

"To the Masucci place?" He waited, watching her eyes, the details of the face he'd gotten to know so well. His heart raced, his gut tightened and everything in him called out to take action. To fix this.

CATHERINE HESITATED. HIS expression was so full of concern she ached for him. It was clear he'd already guessed that the visit hadn't been ideal. In fact, she was sure he knew exactly the kind of reception she'd received.

"I met Deanna. You went to school with her, although she wasn't in your grade."

"Yeah, I know."

"She was very nice. Made coffee. I explained why I hadn't introduced myself before. I mean, I'd made it difficult for anyone to come by, what with me working so much, and the construction. I told her that the noise wouldn't be bad for too much longer. She understood. It was very pleasant. I mentioned the garden, but I learned that her mother grows her own tomatoes. In pots, I think they have a little area in the back of their house."

Catherine turned to the half-finished glass wall and picked up a block. But Tony didn't take the hint— he just kept staring at her. Waiting, she imagined, for the punch line.

"Deanna liked the idea that they'd be able to grow a variety of vegetables. Peppers, lettuce. They cook together, from what she said. She and her family live in the garden apartment, and her mother lives up on the top floor, and they share the main space in the middle. Huh. I wonder how long that's going to last? The mother's getting up there in age. She might not have an easy time with the stairs."

"I take it you met her," Tony said, his voice edged with anger.

Catherine nodded, but she still didn't look at him. "She came home while I was there. She brought Mrs. Soriano with her."

"What did she say to you, Catherine?"

"Nothing. Wanted to know if I'd be flipping the house. But then, everyone assumes I will."

"That's because everyone, including me, is an idiot. Damn it, there's nothing I can do about those old witches. That whole generation feels that they know best about who has the right to live in Little Italy. As if they were the keepers of the keys. Just because their families have lived there a long time doesn't give them any special power. We just have to wait it out. Deal with the fact that they're difficult, and, frankly, mean. Jesus, my own mother and grandmother are hardly models of the kind of neighbors you deserve."

Catherine was surprised. That he'd included his family meant a lot. They had been a little mean. But Tony had been upset enough for both of them, so she'd let it go. It shouldn't have mattered that she understood Italian. People with generous hearts wouldn't say those kinds of things in the first place.

That she didn't figure the whole deal out before she went carrying her cakes to the neighbors stung. Badly. She was a reader of people. An expert. She'd dealt with oligarchs, madmen and heads of state. Her career was built on her ability to make other people understand the real meaning of things when words weren't enough.

Why didn't her gift work in the one place she needed it most? Tony continued to surprise her all the time. As for the old women, they were nothing unusual. There were people like them in every culture. What was wrong with her, that she'd been blindsided? That she let it hurt her so badly?

"Hey," Tony said gently. "There are also a lot of people like Deanna. Like my brothers, like me, who see you for all you bring to this stupid neighborhood. You just happened to have the bad luck to be sandwiched between two of the worst offenders. Even Nonna doesn't like them, and much as I love her, Nonna can be a bitch."

That made Catherine laugh. And lightened up the atmosphere. A bit. Tony was still not happy.

"Don't let them change your plans. You don't have to make a decision tonight. See what Ben has to say, okay? He's an expert at designing gardens that fit the owner's personalitics and nccds."

Tony uncovered the mortar tray and took up his trowel. "I know we've talked about this before, but you can still change your mind about thc basement. It won't have any effect on what we do with your stoop. You've seen a lot of those operations around, with the entrance to the first floor to one side, and the entrance to the store on the other. No one would bother you. And it couldn't hurt as far as the rest of the community is concerned. It would add one more thing that you'd have in common with so many people who live and work here. Just, please don't let it be a bakery. I'd end up huge."

She smiled. He really was trying to make things okay with her. Which was very sweet. And yet she still heard the voice in the back of her mind that said perhaps he could have warncd hcr? No, he had, in his own way, been very forthcoming about the gossip. And maybe the whole dinner with his family was his way of sending up red flags.

The thing was, he'd been so encouraging. Willing to help her. Making it fun to work by his side, working on the kind of projects she never would have on her own. Just Sunday morning he'd told her that she didn't understand the neighborhood. In retrospect, something a bit more specific would've been helpful.

He was staring at her, waiting for a response, she supposed, except she didn't know what to say. "Look,

Catherine, I know it seems weird to you to rent out the basement, but around here—"

"I realize I haven't said much about remodeling that floor, but there's a reason I don't want to rent out the space," she said, pausing only to take a quick, fortifying breath. "I want children, hopefully in the not too distant future, and I'll need more room for them. No one would want to rent there, only to have me kick them out in a couple of years."

With that confession, something eased in her shoulders, at the exact same time her heart nearly beat out of her chest. Shock registered on Tony's face. She waited for just a little smile. Even a blink. On the drive to Cape Cod he'd admitted he wanted children. That wasn't at all the reason she'd told him. It was simply the truth, and it affected the work they were doing.

He kept staring without uttering a single word.

Terrific, she could finally read him.

She had to wonder what it was about her that made her desire for children so surprising. Probably because she was, after all, his temporary lover. Not a girlfriend, and maybe not someone he could foresee becoming his life partner.

She couldn't rule out the possibility that Tony had struck up the intimate relationship with her only because he'd expected her to pack up and leave soon.

Oh, God, she didn't want to believe that of him. And she didn't. No, not Tony. And yet he was still completely dumbstruck.

"Did I just scare you to death?" she asked, hoping he would do something. Smile. Make a joke.

He opened his mouth, and from his expression, it didn't appear he was thinking anything good. But the doorbell interrupted whatever it was. She took advantage of the moment, and hurried to let in the rooftop designer.

TONY STARED AT his computer monitor, finally admitting he'd have to do this budget another time. He hadn't been able to concentrate since he'd left Catherine's last night. He'd been relieved when the doorbell chimed, but as soon as the three of them had gone to the roof, he'd realized the timing couldn't have been worse.

Catherine had no enthusiasm and she'd started the whole conversation by telling Ben she wanted to reduce the garden plans to the bare minimum. Even after Ben had shown her his drawings—geared to her original wishes—she'd been distant. Businesslike. As if they'd been discussing someone else's project.

And what had Tony done? Nothing. He'd stood there, fuming about the damn neighbors, trying to figure out a way to make things right. And when he wasn't cursing the old women, he was thinking about Catherine wanting kids. The way she'd said it so matter-of-factly, she could've been speaking to a coworker about her future. So it was pretty clear she'd meant after he was out of the picture.

God, how they'd needed to talk, but when the three of them had left the rooftop and gone downstairs, she'd said good-night. To both of them.

Once he and Ben were outside, he'd planned on calling her, but Ben asked him about another job, and by the time Tony was alone again, phone in hand, Catherine had turned off all the lights. The temptation to knock on the door was strong, but so were his doubts. Idiot. He shouldn't have let anything stop him.

Luca interrupted his self-flagellation. "Hey, Tony."

"Shut the door."

His brother paused, eyebrows raised, but did as requested. "What's up?"

"I know you're swamped, but if I take over the Maloof project, would you be willing to take over the Fox job?"

Luca sat down across from Tony and immediately put his feet up on the coffee table between him and the desk. "As in Catherine Fox."

"Yes."

"Why?"

"What difference does it make?"

"I doubt that you meant to sound quite that defensive. Come on, Tony. I know you like her. What's wrong? The job? The two of you?"

Tony leaned back in the big black chair. He hadn't felt this lost since he'd realized he might lose his father. "The job's fine. Sal's been on top of everything. There've been remarkably few fuckups. Catherine met with Ben about the rooftop garden, and she's got to make some decisions about what she wants. Also, Dave Rattigan has a lot of her ironwork done, but he needs to make a trip down here to get some measurements."

"He doesn't trust you?"

"He's careful. I appreciate that. He's finished everything but the staircases."

"Look, you can catch me up on the work whenever. But something's bothering the hell out of you, and it's clear that you need to talk about it. It doesn't have anything to do with the trust, does it?"

"Of course not. She doesn't know about it. It's not something I would talk about. Besides, that wouldn't matter to her. She's got money. Look, this is nuts. I'll send you everything about the job and you can walk me through the Maloof—"

"For God's sake, Tony. Stop. Talk to me. Do you want me to get out Dad's bottle of whiskey?"

Tony blew out a breath as he considered. He was damned confused, so maybe Luca was right. He needed to talk to someone. "The neighbors are ruining everything."

"Uh, we all knew that was going to happen."

"No, you don't get it. I had a chance, right at the start, to lay it out for her. I could have explained that some of her neighbors were going to try their best to run her off. That they weren't just delusional, but determined. Christ, why did she have to pick that house?"

"So why didn't you?" Luca asked, moving his feet to the floor so he could lean forward, his elbows on his knees.

"Why didn't I what?"

"Lay it out for her. I mean, once you got to know her."

Either Tony spilled it all or he stopped this conversation right now. He thought briefly about the whiskey, but then gave it up. He needed help. "I knew she'd eventually figure out that she'd be better off flipping the house. Even when she told me she wanted to live there forever, I kept my mouth shut. All she wants is to become part of a community. Unfortunately, a few people can ruin everything."

"There are lots of folks who aren't part of that gang of bullies. People we don't even know that might end up as her best friends."

"But living between those two—"

"Was bad luck, yes. But she seems like a strong person. Once she gets over the disappointment, I bet she'll figure out a way to make it work. So why do you need to leave the job?"

And there it was. "Things between us got…personal."

Luca tried to control a smile. "Yeah, I figured."

Tony huffed. "So everyone knows about us?"

"No one knows. But they're all assuming. You are over there a lot."

Tony stood up. "Shit. I've really fumbled this."

"It's too late to stop talking now," Luca said, in his typical, logical way. "What else?"

Tony walked over to the closed door. Locked it. Didn't turn around. "I've fallen in love with her."

"Okay."

"She told me she wants kids. With some future guy. Who wasn't an idiot for not telling her the complete truth when he had the opportunity."

"She said that? About not wanting kids with you?"

"No. She didn't have to."

Luca sighed. "Come on. It was never going to be easy. Not like it was with Angie. Everyone just expected you to be with her."

Tony turned around and he was pissed. "Exactly. Angie and I took the road of least resistance. But Catherine? I mean, she's...great. She's smart and funny and beautiful. She's everything I didn't know I needed. But—"

"She's not one of us."

"I can't imagine Mom being very happy about the news."

Luca shrugged. "She'll be whatever. If you're determined to live your life trying to be the perfect son, I don't envy you."

"What are talking about?"

"You're not ever going to be Dad. Which is a good thing, by the way. And you're not ever going to please Mom unless you marry another Angie. So? What do you want?"

"That's right, you weren't there that day in the office." Tony smirked. "Mom said it could never have worked with Angie because she was too modern."

Luca laughed. "Seriously?"

"So you can imagine what she'd say about Catherine."

"You know what?" Luca said. "Tough shit."

"Hey, that's how I feel." Tony shook his head. "This isn't about me being the perfect son. I'm worried about Catherine and the crap she'd have to put up with. And I'm not talking about our family. I can handle Mom and Nonna."

"That's up to her to decide. Personally, I don't think you're worth it." Luca shrugged. "But if you don't ask, you'll never know."

"Yeah, thanks." Tony ignored the playful jab, but Luca was right about asking. "I need to stop working with her. So we both can think."

"Agreed."

"And I'm not trying to be Dad. I haven't shied away from making changes starting the day I took over."

Luca stood and faced Tony head-on. "You're doing a great job," he said. "He's proud of you. So is Ma. Take your time with your next move, okay? Be really careful with it. I know how upset you were that it didn't work out with Angie, and you haven't known Catherine for very long."

"Catherine's not like anyone else," Tony said. "You know her parents are diplomats. She's lived all over Europe. She's worldly and sophisticated. I wear a tool belt. She never once suggested we should be anything more to each other."

"So what you're telling me," Luca said, frowning, "is that it was all fun and games until you had to go fall in love, huh?"

"That's about it."

"There's only one thing I am absolutely sure of, big brother," Luca said, putting his hand on Tony's shoulder. "You deserve to be happy. Unconditionally."

Tony closed his eyes. Even if Luca was right, there were no guarantees he'd find that happiness with Catherine.

18

AFTER THE LONGEST Thursday she could ever remember, Catherine left work an hour early, belatedly remembering the workers would still be in her house. She almost wished she hadn't agreed to see Tony. He'd texted her earlier and asked if she'd have dinner with him at an uptown restaurant she'd mentioned two weeks ago.

Part of Sal's crew was finishing up in the living room, but she didn't stop to chat before she went upstairs. The first thing she did was kick off her heels, and the second was pour herself a glass of whiskey. She wouldn't have too much now, since they'd have drinks later, but a few sips of Lagavulin would help her ease into the evening.

That he'd remembered she wanted to go to the Sea Fire Grill was nice, but it wasn't enough. She hadn't slept well, her concentration was shot, and to make matters worse, tomorrow she had to be at work early for a morning meeting. A damned important one for which she couldn't afford to be anything less than at the top of her game.

Yet all she could think about was how quiet Tony had been on the rooftop. He hadn't said a word when she'd told Ben she wanted only the most basic garden.

At first she figured he was still stunned by her admission about wanting children, but she'd been careful not to make it seem as though she expected him to be the father. He'd never given her the impression he wanted that kind of future with her, and even though she'd begun thinking of them that way—well, that was her own fault, wasn't it?

That he'd asked her out was a good sign, though. They could go back to the way things had been before she'd met the neighbors, before she'd put the fear of kids into Tony.

Besides, she wasn't going to let two angry women chase her away. Not from this house. If Belaflore had been here, she'd have given Catherine a hug, then given those two women a lesson in civility they'd never forget.

So, the hell with them. She loved her home, and Tony hadn't been completely scared off, so if she could just get rid of this stupid headache, she was prepared to have a wonderful evening.

Taking her time, she changed, trading her dress for a pair of white linen slacks and a loose fitting charcoal shirt. Not for the first time, she wished she'd realized how inconvenient it would be to leave her master suite until after the kitchen was finished. She was so over being cramped into tight spaces. At least the couch was back in what would be her bedroom when all was said and done.

The drink was already loosening the tension in her shoulders. Tony wouldn't be by until eight, and in the meantime, she wanted to relax. Even though she'd said she wanted only a small garden, she wasn't done thinking that one through. After settling on the couch—her view, a wall decorated by a half dozen paint samples—she gathered up the drawings of the roof-garden plans and put them in order. Ben had been just as creative as she'd been led to believe. The plans were out of this world. He'd taken her through four different versions, from the full community garden/whirlpool tub/pergola/

party space to something completely personal, and he'd made all of them look fantastic.

Damn it, she didn't want to make any cuts. But she also wasn't crazy about the idea of the neighbors having full access to the place.

She'd pictured gatherings with new friends and people from work, harvesting the gardens for the hors d'oeuvres. Now, though? It was too difficult to think about.

After finishing off her drink, she carefully placed the drawings in her tote bag and put on her sandals. She'd check on the progress downstairs, which at the very least would get her out of her own head.

She found two guys in the living room, sanding the newly installed hardwood floor. She'd met them both but didn't think they'd been introduced by name. In the kitchen, Orlando, who was an expert at tile work, was installing the backsplash. He'd made a lot of headway with the glass and pressed tin. But even after he smiled at her, she found her excitement diminished.

Still, it wasn't a reason to be rude. "You're doing a beautiful job, Orlando. It's even better than I'd imagined," she said.

"Thank you. I've never worked with this tin before. It's really nice. I was looking at some tin ceilings online. They used to be really popular."

"Yes, I debated doing the ceiling here. Although it would probably overwhelm the space, especially with the stainless steel appliances."

"You should talk to Luca tomorrow. He's got a really good eye. And we'll be putting in the countertops in the morning, so, you know, you'll get a better feel for what would work."

"Luca's coming tomorrow?"

Orlando nodded. "Sal said he's taken over the project." He went back to placing the glass rectangles on the wall, while she tried hard not to freak out.

Luca was taking over for Tony? For the day? For the rest of the job? He hadn't said anything about that to her when they'd spoken this afternoon. Was that the reason Tony was taking her to dinner in the city?

She was sure, given Orlando's history working on her house, that he hadn't gotten things mixed up. For Luca's name to even enter the conversation meant something was going on.

She left the kitchen and made her way upstairs in a daze. When she'd asked Tony yesterday if she'd scared him away by talking about her future, she'd never imagined… And, God, now the restaurant made sense. Taking her to neutral territory was the perfect place to end things with her.

What else could it be? Perhaps he'd seen the light when she'd told him about her horrible neighbors. In the beginning Tony had been so certain she'd bought the house for the sole purpose of selling it. And if he didn't see a future for the two of them, he might think that her flipping the house would be for the best.

She poured more whiskey and drank it down in one gulp as she thought again about how he'd left last night. He'd walked out along with Ben as if they'd never made plans. After she'd closed the front door, she'd waited, her insides in knots, expecting his knock. But it never came. She'd gone upstairs alone, crawled into bed. Hell, she really had scared him off.

Maybe she should flip the damn house. Why bother making a home where she was so clearly not wanted? She'd make a hell of a profit, sell it to someone who didn't care about fitting in. She had all of Manhattan to choose from for a new home. At least in the heart of the city, she'd be able to find people more like her.

She picked up her empty glass and poured herself another. When she sat down on the couch, she could barely breathe. She'd known the end would come, but not like this. Damn her for letting her feelings for Tony grow. She should have nipped this in the bud after their first night together.

But seeing him tonight? Being forced to listen to all the reasons it made sense for Luca to take over? She couldn't. Not when the reality was twisting her into a mess of sorrow and nerves.

She took another hefty drink and didn't even cough as the single malt burned down her throat. Her purse was in the bedroom, and she got her cell phone out before she chickened out. The urge to text him was tempting. She wasn't entirely sure she could hear his voice without completely falling apart. But no, she was made of stronger stuff than that. She'd just have to keep the call as brief as possible.

It still hurt to hit the speed-dial number.

Tony saw it was Catherine calling, and he immediately saved his spreadsheet, no longer caring much about the budget projections. "Hey," he said, wondering if she was running late. "What's going on?"

"Something's come up at work," she said, her voice different, more clipped and businesslike. "I have to cancel our dinner."

"What? No. I thought…" Damn it. He needed to talk to her tonight. Luca was already planning on showing up at her place tomorrow. "Can I come over when you're done?"

"I have no idea when that would be. Maybe we could

go tomorrow night. This business should be over by then."

"Look, I was hoping… There's been a change. Luca is going to be taking over your renovation starting tomorrow, and I wanted to talk to you about it."

"Taking over for good?"

"Yeah," Tony said, surprised at her mild reaction. "But I want to explain why. In person. Tonight."

"Well, that's…quite a big change, but I'm sorry, I can't discuss it now. I've got people waiting for me. You'll have to tell me tomorrow."

"But I don't want you to think—"

"I'm sorry. I have to go."

"Okay," he said, but she'd already disconnected. This was not good. He'd planned everything out so she'd understand that he wanted more between them than a job contract and a brief affair. She hadn't even sounded that upset, although that could be explained if there were other people with her. She'd been rushed. He didn't understand the details of her job, but this wasn't the first time she'd had to cancel plans at the last minute.

There was no reason to get crazy. He'd talk to her tomorrow. Straighten everything out as soon as possible. Now that he knew what he wanted, he couldn't wait to get started.

Tony had called her four times. Two messages before the meeting and two during. She'd let the messages go to voice mail and hadn't listened to them. Not that she wouldn't; she simply couldn't let anything personal derail her. The meeting had been too important.

That she was in this situation at all wasn't like her. She could practically hear her mother's reaction if she ever found out. *Never show your hand. There's no advantage in letting anyone see your weaknesses.*

Those lessons had been a major part of Catherine's education. It wasn't until she'd gone away to university that she'd really had the opportunity to examine the values of her parents, and eventually to decide to create her own code for living.

The question now was whether to revert to her old self, the self her parents approved of, or continue on her current path, knowing what real heartache felt like.

Her imagination hadn't been up to the task. She'd never really been in love before, although she'd mistaken other things for it. Companionship. Acceptance. Flattery. Hormones.

Twenty-eight years old was far too late to realize how a heart could break. How physical it was. She had entered into this...thing so blithely, swayed by Tony's good looks and charm. In hindsight, it had been a childish choice. She'd know better in the future.

At least now she knew what she was going to do. She'd even taken a rare afternoon off as personal time. As the taxi pulled up in front of her house, she prepared herself to meet with Luca. The conversation wasn't going to take long, and after, she'd finish packing her bags and go check in to The Four Seasons hotel she'd booked. The idea of staying, knowing Tony would never be back, was too much to handle. Besides, she wanted to step up the renovation, no matter what the cost.

As if to solidify her plans, the first person she saw once she was out of the cab was Mrs. Masucci, standing on her stoop. The woman looked right at her, and Catherine nodded politely. There was no acknowledgment of the courtesy. Of course there wasn't. It took all Catharine's willpower not to call out a greeting in Italian.

The moment she walked into the house, she felt the difference. Luca was there; she could hear his voice in the living room, just beyond the foyer. He must have heard the door shut, because he came to meet her, smiling, holding his hand out. He wore a loose blue, button-down shirt over pressed jeans. Nothing Tony would wear. In fact, all she could see were the differences.

She took his hand, grateful that they'd started off on the right business footing.

"It's nice to see you again, Catherine. The house is looking great. I really like what you've done with the restoration."

"Thank you, but I didn't do much. It was very nice of Tony to fill in for George. He's done an excellent job. Why don't we go upstairs, so we can talk."

He nodded, and she led him up the stairs and offered him a seat on the couch. "Can I get you anything? Coffee, soda?"

"I'm good, thanks."

She sat on the other end of the couch and went right for it, not daring to hesitate. "I'd like to make some changes as to how we're going to proceed. I'll be moving into a hotel after we're done with our chat so that Sal and his crew can start work on this floor in earnest. If you could, please notify Ben that I've made my final decision, and that I'd like the minimalist roof garden. I've already seen the plans, and I approve of them.

"Also, if you could find out where Dave Rattigan is on the outdoor staircase, that would be helpful. I'd like to cancel the order if he hasn't started. If not, I'll pay for the work already done, but I won't be installing it." She inhaled deeply, struggling to keep her cool. "I'd also like all the furniture and accessories that are left on this floor to be moved to the basement level..." Her voice cracked, but she'd be damned if she'd blow it now. "And I'll make arrangements for putting them in storage."

She could tell he'd seen her falter, but he quickly reverted to a businesslike stance. "Does this change of direction have anything to do with the quality of our work?"

"Not at all. Paladino & Sons have done everything we agreed upon. I just no longer wish to spend as extravagantly. I'm happy with the current restorations, but I won't be looking to do more, now that the bathroom glass wall is finished."

God, she needed to end this conversation as quickly as possible. Her hands had started to tremble. "I want the house to be appealing, but not over the top. I let myself get carried away, when there's no need."

"Okay. No problem. I'd like to schedule a walk-through with you. Make sure we're on the same page."

"Fine." She pulled her planner from her briefcase, gripping it tightly. "Can you do it tomorrow morning?"

"Of course."

"Great. Thank you." She stood. "I've got to finish packing, so if you don't mind…"

He got a business card from his wallet. "Feel free to call my cell phone direct if you need anything else."

She nodded. Watched him go down the stairs. Ran her hands down her skirt and headed to her bedroom. The moment she saw her two suitcases open on the bed she burst into tears.

THE PACKING WASN'T going well. Not just because she'd been crying for half an hour, although that had a lot to do with it. Also, feeling like an idiot for crying so long was definitely having an effect.

There had been a couple times in her life when she'd

wept over a relationship, but those were dripping faucets compared with Niagara Falls. She'd always thought that girls who completely fell apart over men were ridiculous. Childish. Lacking in self-esteem.

She'd been such a clueless idiot.

What had finally stalled the waterworks had been an errant thought. One that wasn't filled with self-pity. She'd remembered that Tony had wanted to meet with her. To talk to her. Explain why he was calling things off. Like a grown-up.

Pity that in the throes of her drama she'd deleted all his texts and voice mails.

She sniffed, blew her nose again, made herself go into the bathroom and look at the damage she'd done to her face. It was swollen and blotchy and looked as if she was at the tail end of a serious cold. Makeup could hardly hide her state. She should text him. Make arrangements to meet him tomorrow—

Oh, God. What was the matter with her? Once Luca told him about her change of heart, Tony wouldn't wait. And he wouldn't be sending a text. He'd call and, if she didn't answer, he'd show up in person. In fact, knowing him, he could be at her door at any moment.

She started throwing things into her bag. Whatever she forgot she'd pick up later. She had every intention of meeting with him. He'd made an honorable effort to have a face-to-face with her. But right now she had to get out of there. When they finally talked she had to be prepared. Composed. Not a tear left to shed.

Although making him wait for another day seemed like a cruel thing to do to someone who'd done nothing wrong. For 95 percent of their acquaintance he'd been wonderful.

She didn't want to be this person. Now, instead of just

hearing what he had to say, she owed him an apology for taking the weasel's way out of facing the facts.

It was three thirty when she climbed into a cab and headed for her hotel. During the short ride she decided she didn't want to put this off any longer. If not for her heart's sake, then for her own self-respect.

By the time she was safely in her hotel room, she'd calmed down. Her skin wasn't as blotchy anymore and she made up her mind to meet with Tony today and listen to everything he had to say. After he was finished, she'd be gracious, apologize for not calling him sooner and wish him all the best. She hoped he wouldn't ask to still be friends. That wouldn't be possible.

She got out her phone and almost hit speed dial. Swallowing hard, she fished out Luca's business card and found the number for Paladino & Sons. From now on it was just business between her and Tony. Thankfully, the receptionist answered. "Can you tell me if Tony Paladino is working in the office today?"

"Yes, he is, although he's with a client at the moment. Can I take a message?"

"Would you happen to know if he's going to be with clients for the rest of the afternoon?"

"No, it looks like he'll be free from four to five thirty. Would—"

"Thank you," she said, then disconnected. She could be there at four thirty. Hopefully, the receptionist would still be there. But it didn't really matter. This meeting was just business. Catherine was still a client, after all.

"FOR GOD'S SAKE, why didn't you call me after you left Catherine's?"

Luca had just entered Tony's office. As soon as he closed the door behind him Tony's gut clenched.

"I knew you were in with a client and it was kind of hard to leave a message."

"Just tell me what happened." Tony had to force himself to stay in his chair and not shake his brother until he talked.

"Okay. Jesus, this isn't easy."

Luca sat in his usual seat across from Tony, but he was fiddling with a pen, which was something he did only when he was nervous. "She wants to cut everything back. The minimalist garden, no outside staircase. No more restoration."

"Did you tell her I—"

"Me? I acted like a contractor, Tony."

"Did she say why?"

"Not really. Blamed it on getting carried away and spending foolishly, something like that."

"Fuck." Tony rubbed a hand over his hair. "She hasn't answered any of my texts or calls. I tried to explain that I just wanted to take the business part of…us out of the equation. It seemed reasonable, but…" Tony shook his head. Feeling helpless wasn't something he dealt with very well. And with her not talking to him the only thing he could come up with was that she never wanted anything more than what they had. "I know she's out of my league, but I was starting to think it didn't matter so much. Although why wouldn't it? She's a goddamn heiress to some crazy fortune, and I'm—"

"Worth a fortune, too."

"I told you before why we couldn't make it work, and I was right. I got my hopes up, that's all."

"So?" Luca frowned. "That's it?"

Tony blew out a breath, his wayward thoughts and fears making him nuts. "I have to talk to her." He got to his feet. "If she won't answer her phone I'll break down the damn door if I have to."

"Um, you'll have to settle for calling her again."

Something in his brother's voice stopped Tony just as he made it around the desk.

"She was packing when I left," Luca said. "She's moving into a hotel."

Tony's heart nearly quit on him. He stared at his brother. "Which one?"

"Didn't say."

Tony muttered every curse word he knew. In every language he knew. Catherine would've appreciated it. If he hadn't lost her...

Gina buzzed in. "Tony. Your folks are here. Are you two talking about something naughty or can they join you?"

Tony closed his eyes. The last thing he wanted was to see his parents. Why the hell were they even there? He was just about to ask Gina to tell them he'd be tied up for another hour when he heard the doorknob turn. Could his day get any worse?

19

JOE OPENED THE DOOR. "Luca, you're here. Theresa, did you know?"

"No. It's good, though. We just came back from taking a walk and we thought we'd ask you to dinner. Both of you."

"Thanks," Tony said, "but I can't leave right now."

"We're not asking you to," Joe said. "We can go when you're done. We'll rest a bit. She made me walk two miles."

"That's great, Dad." Luca stood up. "Ma, sit here. Dad, take the other chair. You want something to drink?"

Tony wanted to tell all three of them to get the hell out of his office. He didn't give a shit about dinner or something to drink. His insides were twisted with fury at himself and every minute the anger got worse. It had gotten to the point that he didn't know how long he could remain civil.

He should have waited until he'd talked to her before switching out with Luca. He should have found out if she was even interested in him for more than sex and a few laughs. How could he be thirty-three and still this stupid? "Dad, come sit in your chair."

"Your mother doesn't like it. She thinks when I sit there, I'm working."

"He doesn't need to work," Theresa said, "but he saw Sal at the corner today. He said something's wrong with the Fox job. That's all your father could talk about on the walk. So tell him everything's fine and he can sit where he wants."

Tony tried not to react, but that rarely worked with his mother.

"So something is wrong." She sighed, as if the burden was too much to bear.

Luca, always the peacemaker, pulled one of the chairs from the far side of Tony's office and brought it next to his mother's. "Nothing's wrong. She's making some changes, that's all. There's nothing to worry about."

"Nothing to worry about except you're in charge now? What, so she finally admitted she's going to sell?" Theresa poked Joe in the shoulder. "What did I say, huh? She's a smart girl. She knew she could make a fortune on that house. But then she met Tony, so she said she was staying. Now she knows better."

Tony stared at his mother. "She didn't... She wasn't scheming. Catherine wanted to stay, and it had nothing to do with me. But you're right about one thing...now she does know better. She's too damn good for our neighborhood. What the hell kind of people have the right to be so ugly to someone who's cared more about that old house than anyone we've ever worked with? You knew nothing about her, and all you could do was gossip about how this one wasn't Italian and that one wasn't Catholic, and how anyone who wasn't just like us was nothing. And Nonna, telling her right to her face that she would never stand a chance with me? Like I'm better than her?"

"Wait a minute," Joe said. "Nonna would never—"

"Catherine works for the UN. She speaks perfect Italian. She lived in Italy for years."

Theresa's eyes widened. "Why didn't she say?"

Tony slapped his hands on his desk and leaned over stiff arms. "You shouldn't have had to know. You should have been nice to her regardless. Welcoming her like good neighbors would. I swear, between my own family and those judgmental old women who live next door to her, why would she want to stay?"

He slammed his ledger shut, making Joe jump, and walked away from the desk. Tony never spoke to his parents like this, but goddamn it. "And after all the work she's done. She knows more about the history of the building than I do. She could conduct tours at the Tenement Museum, and I know that because I was there when they asked her to. She's studied all the history of the architecture from before our families arrived. Is paying a fortune to restore everything she could about that old house. The fireplaces, the bathrooms, the floors, the tile, the tin plate backsplash in the kitchen. She was making it into something extraordinary."

His mother stared at him as if he'd lost his mind. He walked to the file cabinets and it was tempting as hell to pull out every single drawer and throw them across the room.

"Tony, *tesoro*, what's going on?"

"He's been seeing her," Luca said. "He asked me to take over, so it wouldn't be too complicated."

"Nonna was right?"

Tony faced his mother. "No. Nonna had it backward. I'm the one who thought I'd have a chance with Catherine. She woke me up, Ma. Because of her, I fell in love with this neighborhood again. I was helping her with the restorations, and they were like hidden treasure. All the things we paint over without a thought. She was going to build a roof garden, big enough to share with the families around her. She wanted her neighbors to grow their own vegetables, teach their kids about what a privilege it is to eat things you planted. And you know what else? I tried to talk her into renting out the basement, but she said no. That space was to be filled with her family. With her children. She wanted them to have a legacy. Everything we're doing with the trust, she wanted to do that for her family. In honor of Belaflore Calabrese, who raised her because her parents were too caught up with their own lives.

"And Nonna thinks I'm too good for her? I wasn't just seeing her. I fell in love with her. But I know she can't love me back because—" He had to stop or he was going to lose it. "She should flip the house and get the hell out of this neighborhood."

"Why didn't you tell me?" Theresa said. "I would have—"

"What? Told me how she wasn't Italian? That she was too modern? That I had an obligation to the family?"

Theresa stood up, her face flushed, her eyes worried. "Probably. But I also would have listened to you. I would have seen that you care deeply for this woman. I would have told you to be happy."

"I wish I could believe that," he said.

"Why do you think I didn't push you to stay with Angie? She wasn't right for you. I could see. But it sounds like you think Catherine is."

Tony felt empty. He'd assumed telling his family what he really thought would make him feel better. He sank onto his chair, the weight of despair too heavy. "I think I've just lost the woman I was meant to be with."

"I don't believe that's quite accurate."

Tony looked up at the unmistakable sound of Catherine's voice. She was standing at the open door. Gina was behind her, smiling like the cat that got the cream. Of course she'd been eavesdropping, but he didn't care. Catherine was here.

He slowly got to his feet. "What are you...?"

Catherine smiled. The way she used to smile before everything had started to fall apart. He could see she wasn't at her best. Her eyes looked puffy and her hair was falling down from where she'd pinned it, but he'd never seen anyone more beautiful.

"I came here to talk to you. To listen. Face-to-face. When I heard that you didn't want to work with me anymore, I thought you didn't want to..." She glanced around at his family. "I took it the wrong way."

"No. God no. I didn't want work to come between us. That's all. I wanted to make sure you knew I was serious. That I'd fallen in love with you."

She took a step toward him. "Not exactly the way I pictured the moment, but I'll take it."

Luca coughed. "We're all gonna just leave the office and have some dinner. And Gina's coming with us." He herded Tony's parents toward the door, but his mother hesitated by Catherine.

"Okay, so you're not Italian by birth, but I think you are in your heart. He's a good man, and he deserves someone smart, who can appreciate him. *Hai la mia benedizione.*"

Then Joe touched Catherine's arm. "I liked you that first day. Remember? Now, tell him to make you an honest woman so you can get busy making my grandchildren."

THEY WERE FINALLY ALONE. Just the two of them. And Catherine couldn't manage to make her feet move.

Tony shook his head. "Fair warning. Despite giving us her blessing, my mother's not going to change."

Catherine's heart was beating so fast she probably needed to sit down. After hearing what he'd said about her, she was afraid she might be dreaming. Regardless, she'd never felt braver. "Well, good thing I'm not marrying her."

"I'll say. Wait. Did you just...?"

"Yes. I think I just did."

Oh, the way he looked at her. He took a step and she took a step and they were close enough that she could see the love in his eyes.

He brushed back a tendril of hair that had caught on her lashes. "The answer, if you didn't know already, is yes."

She kissed him lightly on the lips. "That, I could read. Finally."

Tony smiled. "I'll tell you everything you want to know. You'll never have to guess. Starting with the fact that you're the most amazing woman I've ever met. I don't give a damn that you're not Italian. I don't give a damn what my parents think. Or the neighbors. Or anyone else. I love you. I didn't know I could love like this."

Thank God she'd used up all her tears for a lifetime. However, she wasn't so sure her voice would hold up "Me, too," she said finally. "I love you, Tony Paladino. So much it's just a little overwhelming. But about those grandchildren..."

"Ignore him. It's because he's been ill—"

"I don't want to ignore that. But I also want to take some time to just be with you. Out in the open, where everyone can gossip about us as much as they like."

"Excellent plan."

"And also, it doesn't matter, but you should know. My parents aren't going to be all that thrilled."

"What, they don't want a New York contractor for their only daughter?"

"They'll adjust," she said.

"I hope so."

"You know who would be ecstatic about this?"

"Me?"

"Besides you. Belaflore. I think she had you in mind when she told me every single story she could remember about Little Italy."

Tony pulled Catherine even closer, until she put her arms around his neck. "I'm sorry I never met her, and I hope you tell me all those stories, but I have to kiss you now."

"About time," she said.

Then he kissed her. Like in a fairy tale. But even better. Because he was real, and he was hers.

* * * * *

Look for the next book in the fun, sexy
NYC BACHELORS *miniseries*
featuring Luca Paladino.
DARING IN THE CITY
by Jo Leigh is on sale January 2017
wherever Harlequin Blaze books are sold!

COMING NEXT MONTH FROM

HARLEQUIN *Blaze*

Available September 20, 2016

#911 HIS TO PROTECT
Uniformly Hot! • by Karen Rock

Lt. Commander Mark Sampson hasn't been the same since he left one of his rescue swimmers in a stormy sea. Too bad the beautiful stranger he just spent the night with is the man's sister...and a Red Cross nurse assigned to his next mission!

#912 HER HALLOWEEN TREAT
Men at Work • by Tiffany Reisz

If the best way to get over someone is to get under someone else, handyman Chris Steffensen is definitely repairing Joey Silvia's broken heart. But is Joey's high school friend a guy she could really fall for?

#913 THE MIGHTY QUINNS: TRISTAN
The Mighty Quinns • by Kate Hoffmann

Lawyer Tristan Quinn poses as a writer to start a charm campaign against the residents of a writer's colony who are staunchly opposed to selling. But his fiercest—and sexiest—opponent, Lily Harrison, isn't buying it. So he'll have to up his offensive from charm...to seduction.

#914 A DANGEROUSLY SEXY SECRET
The Dangerous Bachelors Club • by Stefanie London

Wren Livingston must hide her identity from her to-die-for neighbor, Rhys Glover, while he investigates the crime she's committed. But hiding her attraction to him proves impossible after one particularly intimate night...

REQUEST YOUR FREE BOOKS!
2 FREE NOVELS PLUS 2 FREE GIFTS!

(H) HARLEQUIN®

Blaze
red-hot reads!

YES! Please send me 2 FREE Harlequin® Blaze® novels and my 2 FREE gifts (gifts are worth about $10). After receiving them, if I don't wish to receive any more books, I can return the shipping statement marked "cancel." If I don't cancel, I will receive 4 brand-new novels every month and be billed just $4.74 per book in the U.S. or $5.21 per book in Canada. That's a savings of at least 14% off the cover price. It's quite a bargain. Shipping and handling is just 50¢ per book in the U.S. and 75¢ per book in Canada.* I understand that accepting the 2 free books and gifts places me under no obligation to buy anything. I can always return a shipment and cancel at any time. Even if I never buy another book, the two free books and gifts are mine to keep forever.

150/350 HDN GH2D

Name _____ (PLEASE PRINT) _____

Address _____ Apt. # _____

City _____ State/Prov. _____ Zip/Postal Code _____

Signature (if under 18, a parent or guardian must sign)

Mail to the **Reader Service:**
IN U.S.A.: P.O. Box 1867, Buffalo, NY 14240-1867
IN CANADA: P.O. Box 609, Fort Erie, Ontario L2A 5X3

Want to try two free books from another line?
Call 1-800-873-8635 or visit www.ReaderService.com.

* Terms and prices subject to change without notice. Prices do not include applicable taxes. Sales tax applicable in N.Y. Canadian residents will be charged applicable taxes. Offer not valid in Quebec. This offer is limited to one order per household. Not valid for current subscribers to Harlequin Blaze books. All orders subject to credit approval. Credit or debit balances in a customer's account(s) may be offset by any other outstanding balance owed by or to the customer. Please allow 4 to 6 weeks for delivery. Offer available while quantities last.

Your Privacy—The Reader Service is committed to protecting your privacy. Our Privacy Policy is available online at www.ReaderService.com or upon request from the Reader Service.

We make a portion of our mailing list available to reputable third parties that offer products we believe may interest you. If you prefer that we not exchange your name with third parties, or if you wish to clarify or modify your communication preferences, please visit us at www.ReaderService.com/consumerchoice or write to us at Reader Service Preference Service, P.O. Box 9062, Buffalo, NY 14240-9062. Include your complete name and address.

HB15

*If the best way to get over someone is to get under
someone else, handyman Chris Steffensen is definitely
repairing Joey Silvia's broken heart. But is Joey's high
school friend a guy she could really fall for?*

*Read on for a sneak peek from
HER HALLOWEEN TREAT, the first in a special holiday-
themed trilogy from bestselling author Tiffany Reisz.*

"I'm going to go up and see what he's doing," Joey saw a
large green Ford pickup parked behind the house with the
words *Lost Lake Painting and Contracting* on the side in
black-and-gold letters.

"I'll stay on the line," Kira said. "If you think he's
going to murder you, say, um, 'I'm on the phone with my
best friend, Kira. She's a cop.' And if he's sexy and you
want to bang him, just say, 'Nice weather we're having,
isn't it?'"

"It's the Pacific Northwest. In October. It's forty-eight
degrees out and raining."

"Just say it!

"Now, go check him out. Try not to get murdered."

Joey crept up the stairs and found they no longer
squeaked like they used to. Someone had replaced the old
stairs with beautiful reclaimed pine from the looks of it.

"Hello?"

"I'm in the master," the male voice answered.

Joey walked down the hallway to a partly open door.

There on a step stool stood a man with dirty-blond hair cut neat and a close-trimmed nearly blond beard. He was concentrating on the wiring above his head. He wore jeans, perfectly fitted, and a red-and-navy flannel shirt, sleeves rolled up to his elbows.

"Hey, Joey," he said. "Good to see you again. How's Hawaii been treating you?"

He turned his head her way and grinned at her. She knew that grin.

Oh, my God, it was Chris.

Chris Steffensen. Dillon's high school best friend. That Chris she wouldn't have trusted to screw in a lightbulb, and now he was wiring up a ceiling fan? And seemed to be doing a very good job of it.

"Did you...did you fix up this whole house?" she asked, rudely ignoring his question.

"Oh, yeah. I'm doing some work for Dillon and Oscar these days. You like what we did with the place?"

He grinned again, a boyish eager grin. She couldn't see anything else in the world because that bright white toothy smile took over his face and her entire field of vision. He was taller than she remembered. Taller and broader. Those shoulders of his...well, there was only one thing to say about that.

Joey hoped Kira was still listening.

"Nice weather we're having, isn't it?"

Don't miss HER HALLOWEEN TREAT by Tiffany Reisz, available October 2016 wherever Harlequin® Blaze® books and ebooks are sold.

www.Harlequin.com

HBEXP0916

Reading Has Its Rewards

Earn **FREE BOOKS!**

Register at **Harlequin My Rewards** and submit your Harlequin purchases from wherever you shop to earn points for free books and other exclusive rewards.

Plus submit your purchases from now till May 30th for a chance to win a $500 Visa Card*.

Visit **HarlequinMyRewards.com** today

MYR16R1

HARLEQUIN®

A Romance FOR EVERY MOOD™

Love the Harlequin book
you just read?

Your opinion matters.

Review this book on your favorite
book site, review site, blog or your own
social media properties and share
your opinion with other readers!

JUST CAN'T GET ENOUGH?

Join our social communities
and talk to us online.

You will have access to the latest
news on upcoming titles and special
promotions, but most importantly,
you can talk to other fans about your
favorite Harlequin reads.

Harlequin.com/Community

HARLEQUIN®

A *Romance* FOR EVERY MOOD™

Stay up-to-date on all your
romance-reading news with the
Harlequin Shopping Guide,
featuring bestselling authors, exciting new
miniseries, books to watch and more!

The newest issue will be delivered right to you
with our compliments! There are 4 each year.

Signing up is easy.

EMAIL

ShoppingGuide@Harlequin.ca

WRITE TO US

HARLEQUIN BOOKS
Attention: Customer Service Department
P.O. Box 9057, Buffalo, NY 14269-9057

OR PHONE

1-800-873-8635 in the United States
1-888-343-9777 in Canada

Please allow 4-6 weeks for delivery of the first issue by mail.